FATAL BY DESIGN

A BOW STREET DUCHESS MYSTERY
BOOK FIVE

CARA DEVLIN

First Cup Press

ALSO BY CARA DEVLIN

The Bow Street Duchess Mystery series

MURDER AT THE SEVEN DIALS

DEATH AT FOURNIER DOWNS

SILENCE OF DECEIT

PENANCE FOR THE DEAD

———

The Sage Canyon series

A HEART WORTH HEALING

A CURE IN THE WILD

A LAND OF FIERCE MERCY

———

THE TROUBLE WE KEEP

A Second Chance Western Romance

CHAPTER
ONE

August 1820

The halls of Greenbriar buzzed with activity. Footmen and maids moved swiftly, unrolling recently cleaned carpets, arranging flowers in numerous vases, dusting and sweeping and polishing, and whatever else Mrs. Dorman, the housekeeper, ordered necessary for the coming house party and its guests. The flock was to begin arriving that afternoon. By then, however, Audrey would be gone.

She walked alongside her sister-in-law toward the manor's front entrance, though she suspected Genie's ambling gait was purposefully slowing their progress.

For at least the sixth time since breakfast, Genie said, "You are not obliged to leave," and tightened her grasp on their linked arms until she was practically holding Audrey back from taking her next step. "I don't give a fig what anyone might say about your presence. This is my home, my house party, and if I say you are welcome, then no one will contest me."

She had been harping on this point for a few days now, ever since Audrey had announced that it was high time for her to remove to Fournier Downs. She ought not to have even been at her brother- and sister-in-law's Kent estate to begin with, and she certainly should have departed well before the day the guests were to arrive. But Michael and Genie were difficult to argue with. They'd insisted she come stay with them for the summer at Greenbriar, a tract of five thousand acres of rolling fields and farms, woodland, hills, and ponds. The offer had been attractive. Much more so than spending the summer months in Hertfordshire at Fournier Downs, alone. And as the house party approached, with its dozen guests planning to stay a fortnight, Genie and Michael had kept finding reasons for her to remain. Their ultimate hope was that she would stay for the house party too, but it simply could not be done.

"I wish I could, truly." Audrey squeezed Genie's arm. "But you know my presence is impossible. I may be apt to break the rules now and again, but mourning customs are inflexible things."

It had been just over four months since Philip followed through with his plan to "convalesce" in the south of France, accompanied only by his valet, Grayson. Four months since Audrey had clung to him in a final embrace in their London home on Curzon Street, her eyes filled with tears of both heartache and fury.

"I vow to you," he'd whispered as he'd held her. "I will find a way to get word to you when things have settled. Whatever you choose to do from here, with your life, I will not interfere. Ever."

Her throat had been so thick with emotion that she hadn't been able to respond. He'd kissed her forehead, whispered that he loved her, and then departed in his carriage for Dover, where he'd take a packet across the Channel, to Calais. A little over three months ago, the letter she'd dreaded receiving had arrived.

She'd known to expect it but had hoped Philip would change his mind at the last minute. That he would decide to come home after all.

"It is absurd," Genie sighed, though with a note of resignation. "I think it is cruel that we must shut ourselves away from the world during a time like this, when it is companionship and diversion that we most need."

Audrey agreed wholeheartedly but, as she had for the last three months, bit her tongue. She was trapped, it seemed, in an unending miasma of mourning, guilt, and anger. And yet there was the silver lining of possibility, too. Because legally, and in the eyes of king and country, Philip Sinclair, the Duke of Fournier, was dead. She, Audrey Sinclair, the Duchess of Fournier, was a widow. A dowager duchess now, in fact.

But it was all a lie, and Audrey feared she would never be free from it.

"I need no entertainment, Genie. You, Michael, and little George, of course, have been an excellent diversion this summer," she assured her sister-in-law, the new Duchess of Fournier.

Michael, as the second son and spare heir, had only recently been granted the title of duke. What could have taken the House of Lords months, even a year, to declare Philip dead and pass along the title, had taken a much shorter time than usual. The fact that there had been no body recovered had concerned some members of the House—perhaps the duke was only missing. Perhaps he had not drowned off the shores of Marseille when a storm had rushed in, churning the seas, and sweeping away the duke, as his valet Grayson and several witnesses on the beach had reported. For Philip was a strong swimmer, as Michael proclaimed when he was in denial that his brother was gone. He might have washed ashore elsewhere. Dashed his head and lost his memory.

A weeks' long search was launched, but he was not found. After two months, a consensus among the House was reached: the duke was dead.

It was just as Philip had required: a death where his body would not and could not be returned to England for burial. He'd gone through with it—the proverbial nail in the coffin. There could be no coming back from this lie, and before he'd left, he had vowed more than once that he would never attempt it. That he would never endanger whatever future Audrey made for herself by returning and exposing himself as alive and well. Though there had been many times when Audrey had wished to fall asleep and wake up miraculously five months in the past. Once arrived, she would try again to change Philip's mind.

Although, five months in the past would make it the month of March, and the events of that month had been wretched and heartbreaking. Audrey had helped to solve the murder of Miss Eloisa Neatham and prove Bow Street officer

Hugh Marsden innocent of the crime, which had revolved around the illegitimacy of his half-siblings and an incestuous relationship that still made Audrey's stomach clench with revulsion whenever she thought of it.

She and Genie stepped onto the crushed gravel circle in front of Greenbriar, and Audrey breathed in deeply. Surely, to Genie, she appeared to simply be taking in the fresh, mid-August air, heavy with the scent of freesia and rose from the garden beds trimming the exterior brick. But in truth, Audrey often found it difficult to breathe whenever she thought of Philip.

Or of Hugh, for that matter—though for entirely different reasons.

The itch to be on her way caused her waiting barouche-landau, her trunks loaded onto the back rack, to look like it was miles away rather than a few yards, and Genie's pulling arm, like an anchor. Audrey wasn't eager to be alone at Fournier Downs, but her spacious, empty home in Hertford-shire was vastly preferable to the one house party guest whom she would most like to avoid: the new Viscount Neatham. Better known to Audrey as Hugh Marsden.

"Cassie will be upset to have missed you," Genie said.

Philip's younger sister had spent all of June with them at Greenbriar but had been in Brighton for most of July with a party of friends. It was good for her to be out with other ladies and young gentlemen, though of course properly chaperoned by the mothers of two of her companions.

Cassie had been through much turmoil the last year, after finding herself compromised and with child after an earl's son and heir had made sport of her. The cad promised her a betrothal, though he'd never had any intention of following through. Her child, born in secret in Sweden, had been adopted by a family in Stockholm, and Cassie had spent the last several months back in England attempting to regain her footing here, and her happiness.

"Don't you dare allow her to come to Hertfordshire," Audrey replied. It was exactly what Cassie would suggest. "She should stay for the house party. I'm sure she is longing to see William after being so long in Brighton."

Genie's youngest brother had been courting Cassie since the spring. Michael had yet to discuss formal betrothal matters with William, but Audrey was certain the discussion would unfold in the next fortnight, during the party. While not titled, William was a gentleman, and being Genie's brother lent him firmer footing with Michael. He would not be marrying Cassie just for her substantial dowry, that was assured.

But now, Genie's face fell. "He isn't coming."

"I thought he'd accepted the invitation."

"He had. Unfortunately, he has business that will keep him in London."

Audrey frowned at the announcement. There was something more to the story. She could sense Genie holding back. But just then, Audrey's driver bowed as they arrived at the carriage. "Your Graces," Carrigan said, greeting them both.

As dowager duchess, the form of address still applied to Audrey, though sharing it with Genie did feel a little awkward. Her sister-in-law felt the strangeness of it too; though she was now duchess, she had not wanted to push Audrey out of her title or what was due to her. Fournier Downs, for instance. It was the country seat for the Duke of Fournier, but Genie had insisted to Michael that they not remove from Greenbriar until the following summer, after Audrey's year of mourning. Genie's gentle kindness was genuine and a rare thing among the women of the *ton*. A rise in status was certainly something many lords and ladies coveted, though Michael and Genie had not shown even a sliver of happiness for their ascension. They would have much rather had Philip than a ducal title.

"We are ready to depart, Your Grace," Carrigan announced, and then opened the carriage door.

"You know, we are expecting Lord Neatham," Genie said, her wistful, easy tone, entirely put on. Genie was so naturally artless that Audrey knew when she was plotting.

"As I have heard," Audrey replied, arching a brow at the new duchess. "Several times, in fact."

Genie had been in raptures when Hugh accepted her invitation—the very first gathering the newly established viscount had accepted that summer. The whole of the *ton* was utterly fascinated by the former principal Bow Street officer who, during the course of solving his half-sister's murder, also unearthed the truth of his own birth—he was heir to the Neatham title, not his half-brother, Bartholomew. After being reviled by polite society for being the viscount's illegitimate ward, then having baseless accusations of ruining Eloisa heaped onto him, only to then shoot and maim Bartholomew in a duel, Hugh was less than eager to take his title. He'd also been ousted from his post at Bow Street. Accepting society invitations had not been top of list when she'd last seen him, in March.

"Are you not curious as to how he is faring?" Genie asked as Carrigan waited.

Genie was somewhat aware of Audrey's history with

Hugh, though perhaps not of her attachment to him. He had helped to exonerate Philip in a murder case, and then he had helped solve a case at Fournier Downs the previous summer. Most recently, Genie and the rest of society learned that Hugh had saved Audrey's life in Hyde Park when Thomas—Hugh's other half-sibling—had intended to kill her. She'd discovered Thomas was Eloisa's murderer, and he had wanted to silence Audrey too. But Genie couldn't know the rest: that she and Hugh had been valiantly attempting to suppress what had begun as an attraction between them, and had since developed into deeper, more serious feelings.

The truth was, Audrey had fallen irrevocably in love with Hugh, and she was frightened that with his new title, everything had changed.

"I'm sure I will hear all there is to know about the viscount," Audrey said, forcing a grin. "Cassie won't be able to resist filling pages upon pages with gossip for me."

Genie sighed. "Very well. I suppose you should be off. You're fortunate in some ways, you know. The men will all be talking business and money-making ventures, and the ladies will require much entertainment." She frowned. "Remind me again why I am hosting this party."

Audrey laughed and embraced her sister-in-law. Genie lingered in her hold just long enough for Audrey to twitch with worry—Hugh could arrive any moment. But then, Audrey was being handed up into the carriage, the door was closing, and she and her maid, Greer, were swaying to the bounce of the chassis as they rolled down Greenbriar's long lane toward the main road.

They sat on opposite benches in the four-person barouche-landau and rode in companionable silence for a quarter hour or so. Greer had been her lady's maid for four years now, ever since Audrey married Philip. She was attentive and quiet, and steadfastly loyal, and she likely knew all her mistress's many secrets: from Audrey and Philip's marriage arrangement to Philip's non-conformist attraction to men to the fact that Audrey had spent time in an insane asylum—though perhaps she did not know why Audrey's mother and uncle had sent her there. Very few people knew that she could hold objects and see their memories playing out in her mind. Hugh was one of the few who did know. And on that note, Audrey also suspected that Greer was aware of her feelings toward the new viscount.

Just thinking of him as *viscount* unsettled her, though she couldn't entirely explain why. She was far more comfortable thinking of him as Officer Marsden. Or just Hugh. And she thought of him too often.

As much as she missed him, and as much as the opportunity to see him at Greenbriar had been a magnetic temptation, she knew that if she stood face to face with him, she would not be able to lie about Philip. It had been different in their written correspondence in May. Hugh had sent his condolences, offering kind words about Philip, but had not come to Violet House where Audrey had, as required, closed herself off. He could not have come, of course, though she had wondered nearly a dozen nights in a row if he would scale the broad limbs of the tree outside her bedroom window and slip in, undetected, as he had once before, when he'd been evading arrest.

Her brief reply to his letter had been properly distant. Setting anything down in ink about Philip's true whereabouts would have been categorically stupid. Everyone

believed the reports from the Marseille authorities and
Philip's valet Grayson, about the sudden storm at sea.
Grayson's knowledge of the truth and his complicity in
Philip's ultimate plan was almost a given, considering the
valet had written to Barton, the butler at Violet House,
shortly after, resigning his post. He had not returned to
England, as far as she was aware.

"Will you miss Greenbriar?" Audrey asked Greer after
the silence began to wear on her. Too often now, silences
bothered her. They allowed her mind to reel and spin with
things she would rather not think of.

Her maid's lips stretched into a constrained smile.
Greer was not one to show emotion; she was reserved and
thoughtful, and Audrey had often thought that had she
been born into a family of wealth and influence, she would
have made a better lady than half the women in the
peerage.

"I will, Your Grace. I enjoy the staff, and it is such a beautiful residence."

"More beautiful than Fournier Downs, certainly,"
Audrey said. When Greer began to deny it, Audrey only
shook her head. "It is the truth, and I promise that you won't
insult me by agreeing. If I were Their Graces, I would deign
Greenbriar the new—"

A shout and a sharp whistle from the box cut off
Audrey's statement. Carrigan was at the reins, and a footman
was riding along, mostly for protection. The drive from Kent
to Hertfordshire would take them north of London, then
along post roads, and they would not reach home until after
nightfall. Truly, they should have left much earlier. Having a
footman along with Carrigan would be safer. Audrey

couldn't help but think that Hugh would heartily approve the choice.

The carriage slowed.

"Is there a problem?" she called.

"A coach ahead on the road, Your Grace."

Audrey's pulse increased. In March, she and Carrigan had been driving through Hyde Park when he'd stopped to assist another carriage stuck in mud—or at least that is what Thomas, Colonel Trenton, had said to gain Audrey's driver's attention and aid. It had been a ruse. He'd ended up knocking Carrigan unconscious and chasing Audrey through the darkened park.

"A man is hurt," Carrigan now said. Then, as the chassis shook with his and the footman's descent from the box, he added, "If you will stay in the carriage, Your Grace."

She shifted to peer out the open window. The barouche-landau's collapsible roof had been raised for the long drive to Hertfordshire, as the road dust would have coated them crown to foot otherwise. The coach that Carrigan had spotted—a stately deep maroon conveyance hitched to a pair of fine black horses with white stockings—had stopped along the country lane, parallel to a grassy field, and beyond that, a stretch of woodland. It was likely still Greenbriar property, as they had not driven far from Michael and Genie's manor.

A gasp lodged in her throat at the sight of a man slumped over in the driver's box. Dismissing Carrigan's request to stay within the carriage, she opened the door.

"Hand me down, Greer." She turned to lower her foot onto the carriage step, and with her maid's firm hand, nimbly descended to the road. Audrey helped her maid down next.

Together, they rushed across the dusty dirt road.

Carrigan tried to hold them back, his face starker than its usual ruddy appearance.

She immediately saw why.

The man in the driver's box was dead. His hat had toppled to the road, leaving his head bare and the sickly dark hole in the center of his forehead visible. Blood streamed from the wound.

"He's been shot," Greer gasped.

Audrey's limbs began to tingle, and her ears to chime. The coach door was open, and pure dread filled her at what might await them inside.

"Travers, take a look," Carrigan ordered, and guiltily, Audrey felt relief that the footman would be first to peer in. Travers showed no hesitation as he went. He then shook his head.

"Empty," he announced.

Her breaths came faster. Yet again, she'd come upon a dead body. From previous unfortunate experience, she knew not to panic. Audrey stepped back and noticed three things right away. First, the brake on the coach had been engaged, meaning the driver had stopped his team before he'd been killed. Second, a flight of three steps sat had been unfolded and lowered for whoever had been traveling inside. And third, luggage was still secured in the rear rack.

"Someone has left without their possessions," Audrey said, moving toward the open door with more ease now that Travers had assured them there was not another victim inside.

Audrey took the few steps up to investigate while Carrigan instructed Travers. He was to stay here with the coach and the deceased driver, and Carrigan would take the dowager duchess and Greer back to the manor so that he could fetch help. It was a good plan, but Audrey hesitated. Whatever had occurred here, it had been recent. She eyed the crystal hand knob on the open door. Who had descended from this coach, and under what circumstances?

Though she knew she might see a violent encounter, it was the only way to glean facts about what had happened. Audrey peeled off her glove and reached for the knob. She drew in a deep breath and opened her mind.

The empty coach before her dissolved, and a new reality spread out before her like the blooming of ink on paper. A commotion unraveled before her eyes as the energy the door-knob retained transformed into images only Audrey could see. Shock stiffened her arms and legs, and her fingers clutching the knob turned to stone. Two women—a lady and her maid—were being held at gunpoint, both recoiling with fear. Carrigan's entreaties for Audrey to come away from the coach drowned beneath the gasps and yelps of distress from the two women. The sounds were muted and muffled, like vibrations through water, as most sounds in her visions were. So, too, were the commands from a masked man to hand over a ring. The lady screeched that she did not have it, shaking her head and breaking into sobs. As the retained energy in the crystal knob depleted and grew fainter, so did the images.

"Your Grace, please." She felt a touch to her elbow. Audrey gasped as she released the knob and spun away from the interior of the coach. Carrigan and Greer, along with the footman, all stood there, staring at her with concern.

"What is it?" Greer asked at Audrey's alarmed expression.

"I recognize the coach," she lied, because she had to say

something to account for conveying what she had just learned. What she had just seen.

For the lady being accosted had been as familiar to Audrey as her own reflection in the mirror.

"This is Lady Redding's coach," she said. "My sister...I think she has been abducted."

CHAPTER TWO

"The two of you promised you'd be on your best behavior."

Basil slowly turned from staring out at the passing countryside, to glare at Hugh in a way no typical valet would ever dare glare at their employer. Then again, Hugh had long since accepted the fact that Basil was not a typical gentleman's valet. He was an incurable snob with exacting standards, dry wit, and a brassy attitude.

"I am not a petulant child," Basil replied, sounding exactly like a petulant child. Hugh refrained from pointing that out.

"I expect you and Sir to get along and not give the servants at Greenbriar any reason to gossip about the two of you butting heads like a pair of stubborn rams."

Basil sniffed. "I don't know what you mean. We are getting along famously."

Beside the valet, Sir slouched in his seat with his arms crossed and his legs splayed wide. Though he wore a bespoke suit of Neatham livery—buff breeches and waistcoat, topped

by a green and buff coat trimmed with darker green braid—
the boy had a long way to go before he carried himself like a
lord's "assistant". Case in point: the slingshot Sir currently
gripped loosely in one hand.

"I was only attempting to say," Basil continued, "that it is
critical that a servant's facial bearing be passive."

"Stop carping about my face, Baz, or I'll give you a reason
to carp about yours." Sir brandished the slingshot that he'd
been using all afternoon to take aim at squirrels and birds
through the window.

"Your childish toy doesn't threaten me," Basil said.

"Your front teeth'll be saying something different in a
minute," Sir grumbled.

Hugh smothered a snort of laughter. The boy was
around twelve years of age, but coming from the poverty-
stricken slums of Whitechapel, he'd needed to grow up faster
than usual. Street smart and appropriately cautious, Sir had
refused to give Hugh his name when he'd started running
messages for him and bringing him tips on crimes Hugh
might want to investigate. So, he'd taken to calling the boy
Sir. It had stuck.

Of course, now he knew his Christian name—Davy
Givens—but the boy preferred Sir, and Hugh had to admit
he did as well.

"All right, all right, the pair of you, leave off," Hugh said.
"And Sir, put away that thing. You'll not need it at
Greenbriar."

They were coming upon the new Duke of Fournier's
country estate after a full day of road travel from the
Neatham country seat near Cranleigh in Surrey, and they
were all itching to get out and stretch their legs. Though he'd

agreed to attend the house party, he'd been dreading it for weeks, and for more than one reason. Ever since the spring, when Hugh had taken on the mantle of Viscount Neatham, he'd been in a state of turmoil. Inside, he still felt like the old Hugh: the illegitimate ward of the late viscount, the exiled scapegrace accused of ruining his own half-sister and summarily shooting and maiming his half-brother in a duel, and the man who rose from a foot patrolman to principal officer with the Bow Street Runners. But now, at least on the outside, he was no longer most of those things.

No longer illegitimate, he had been identified as the true Neatham heir. It was a title he had never wanted and still wished had not been granted to him. When he'd set out to find his half-sister's murderer last March, he had never imagined what more he'd discover. But revealing Eloisa's killer had also teased out the truth about Hugh's birth, and once brought to light, it could not be shoved back into the shadows. Had there been a way to let Barty keep the title, Hugh would have been delighted to do so. He missed being a principal officer. He missed being Mr. Hugh Marsden. Hell, he missed *not* being a peer.

"Sir, remember—you will not address the duke or duchess directly," Hugh said placidly, so as not to upset the boy or sound accusing. "I understand you have addressed the previous duchess in the past, and she did not mind, but this duchess most certainly will. Is that understood?"

The boy narrowed his eyes with an expression that said, *What am I, a bloody idiot?* He wasn't. Not in the least. On top of Sir's street education, which had given him skills no gently raised boy in the ton would ever gain, Hugh had implemented tutoring lessons these last few months: mathematics, elocution, geography, and much to Sir's discontent, literature. The boy could barely read a primer, but his tutor, Mr. Fines, updated Hugh regularly and claimed he was coming along well.

He half expected Sir was threatening Mr. Fines with that slingshot to report as much, but there was no evidence of it, so Hugh shrugged it off.

"Yes, *my lord*." Sir dragged out the appropriate address with the same sarcasm that had netted him Hugh's respect.

He only hoped Sir would refrain from showcasing his ill temper with the other house party guests and servants for the next fortnight. The length of the social gathering loomed before him like a fathomless abyss. He'd declined countless social events that summer, instead preferring to be alone in Surrey at his country estate, Cranleigh Manor. But when the invitation arrived, embossed with the Fournier name and coat of arms, he'd held the fine linen paper a little longer than necessary.

When news arrived in May that Philip, the Duke of Fournier, had died while visiting the Continent, Hugh's initial reaction had been shameful. He'd despised himself ever since. The fact that Audrey was free from her sham of a marriage had filled him with joy and relief. Belatedly, after cursing himself for his selfishness, he'd recognized that Audrey's dearest friend was dead and that she was surely grieving his loss. They might not have been in love romantically, but they had loved one another as friends.

The longing to go to her and comfort her had crossed his mind, and he'd nearly given in several times before reason won out—that and a scolding command from his friend Grant Thornton, who had paid Hugh a visit with the sole purpose to grab him by the scruff of the neck and warn him against such a show of impropriety.

A Bow Street officer might have been able to get away with climbing up the tree next to Violet House and sneaking into her room at night, but Hugh Marsden, the Viscount Neatham, most certainly could not.

As if he'd needed one more reason to curse his bloody title.

He'd settled for a written letter of condolences, which had read hollow and unfeeling, no matter how many drafts he'd crumpled and tossed into the fire. Audrey had replied with a brief letter of appreciation and equally hollow inquiries as to how he was settling in as viscount. After one more exchange of letters, all communication had ceased.

It was for the best. She was in mourning. Ironically, that made her even more off-limits than she had been before.

The new coach—one of the items that Hugh had not minded selecting and outfitting with four new horses purchased at Tattersall's—slowed as it turned up a long lane. On the left, thick woods hemmed in the lane, and on the right, a perfectly manicured lawn sloped toward a body of water large enough to be deemed a lake rather than a pond. His stomach, which had already been in a knotted state, cinched tighter.

She would not be here.

In her last letter, Audrey had written that she'd be spending the summer at Greenbriar, but Hugh knew she could not attend the house party. Mourning rules forbade it. His longing to set eyes on her again had not diminished, but as the weeks, then months, progressed, that longing had started to change. With it now came uncertainty—that as soon as their eyes met, she would know his despicable, opportunistic thoughts regarding the duke.

Philip had not been a bad man or a terrible husband; he'd not deserved to die, and Hugh had never wished him dead. Not even in his weakest moments, when he considered that the duke's death would be the only way Audrey could be free for another. For *him*. But now that it had come to pass, he worried she might suspect he did feel selfishly happy.

But no, she would not be here, and Hugh would be among others who could inform him as to how she was faring. If the late duke's youngest sibling, Lady Cassandra, was present, she would certainly be eager to divulge everything having to do with her sister-in-law.

The coach turned, giving Hugh a view of the main house at Greenbriar—a large and stately Georgian home with pale rose brick and cream decorative quoins at the corners, giving the impression that the sides of the home had been stitched up like a tailor's seam. Rumor had it that the new duke and duchess had not wanted to turn Audrey out of Fournier House in Hertfordshire and take their rightful place there. It was kind of them. However, seeing Greenbriar now, Hugh also wondered if Michael and his wife, Geneva, were loath to leave their own country seat. It was a beautiful spot; with the lawn sloping to the lake, the prospect from the home was slightly finer than the one at Fournier House.

The coach drew to a stop in the circular courtyard of crushed gravel. Hugh eyed Sir and his bare head. "Cap."

The boy grumbled and picked up the tricorne from his lap, then slapped it onto his head of unruly black curls. Until Hugh had sided with Basil and insisted that Sir bathe regularly now that he was a viscount's assistant, his hair had been perpetually lank and greasy. The curls that had appeared when his hair was clean had been quite the surprise.

So, too, was Sir's attempt to school his features into a complacent expression as the groom descended to open the door. He practically succeeded. Hugh bit back a grin as the door swung open. Almost instantly, a commotion burst through the columned entrance to Greenbriar.

Three footmen wearing plum and silver livery, and a man Hugh presumed to be the butler, hurried toward the coach with more enthusiasm than his arrival warranted. When Michael, the duke himself, came through the open front door with a brisk stride and a grim mien, Hugh understood: Something was wrong.

"Your Grace," Hugh said warily as he came down onto the crushed rock. Tension stewed in the new Duke of Fournier's eyes.

"Excellent timing, Neatham. I'm sorry to meet you with such urgency after your many hours of travel, but it cannot be helped." Fournier quickly directed the footmen and Munson, his butler, to see to Hugh's trunks and staff. Then, he turned back to Hugh. "If you'll follow me."

Fournier was the opposite of the late duke: a few inches shorter, far broader in the shoulder and torso, and dark haired, he came across as decisive and athletic, where his elder brother had exuded reason, calm, and intelligence that had, Hugh thought, often walked the edge of arrogance. It would be difficult to think of this man as *Fournier*. As duke. Then again, it was likely no more difficult than Fournier now having to address Hugh as Lord Neatham. They had both had a change of situation thrust upon them.

"What is this about, Your Grace?" Hugh asked as they entered the home and a large entrance hall.

"Fournier will do," he replied tersely. Hugh wondered if it was because he was as uncomfortable with "Your Grace" as Hugh was with "my lord". The two of them were barely acquaintances; in fact, the last time he'd seen Fournier had been after the late duke's arrest two Aprils ago. They had been at odds then and for good reason. Hugh had locked up his brother for murder.

Fournier came to a stop in the middle of the hall and turned, hands clasped behind his back. He lowered his voice. "There has been an incident on the road leading north, toward Hertfordshire. My sister-in-law's carriage was traveling in that direction when her driver spotted an abandoned coach." Hugh's attention sharpened at the mention of Audrey. "The driver had been shot. Killed."

His skin prickled. "She is unharmed?"

Fournier pressed his lips tightly and nodded. "Shaken. There is more—she claims the conveyance belongs to her sister, Lady Redding, but the lady and anyone she may have been traveling with were no longer within the coach."

Fournier gestured for him to continue following, and then led him through the hall, toward a pair of closed doors. Two footmen opened them, allowing them to enter without slowing. The drawing room, done in pale shades of salmon, currently held four people. Only one of them mattered to Hugh right then.

Audrey stood across the drawing room at the open door to the terrace, her black gown somber against the feminine pink surroundings. She met Hugh's stare, dropped her arms from where they'd been crossed at her waist, and the room and everyone else in it became nonexistent. Distress rendered her cerulean eyes glassy, and they cut into him. The deep blue was even brighter against the contrasting widow's black; her blonde hair, artfully drawn up and pinned, even paler. Hugh drank in the sight of her, momentarily forgetting the reason for her presence. He felt her presence like the wavering push and pull of a lodestone.

"May I introduce my wife, Her Grace, Geneva." Miraculously, the duke's deep voice pierced the bubble that had formed around Hugh and Audrey, at least in his own mind.

Hugh turned to greet the new duchess, a pretty woman of about thirty. She gave him a kind and welcoming smile that faltered.

"Lord Neatham, welcome to Greenbriar. I wish your arrival was not met with such alarming news." She gestured toward Audrey. "You are acquainted with the dowager duchess."

He attempted to keep the depth of their acquaintance from being evidenced on his expression when he looked at Audrey.

"Yes." He sketched a short bow. "Your Grace."

"My lord," she replied, the words breathy and soft. Uncertain. Whether she was simply shaken by the events that had just unfolded, or if his presence bothered her, wasn't clear.

"And this is the duke's brother, Lord Tobias Sinclair," the new duchess continued, placing her hand on the arm of the young man standing at her side. Tobias, the youngest of the Sinclair siblings, was tall, dark-haired, and handsome. Just out of university, most likely.

"It is a pleasure to meet you, Lord Neatham," Lord Tobias said. "My sister speaks highly of you."

Hugh dipped his head in acknowledgement. He and Lady Cassandra had met the previous summer at Fournier Downs. She'd been spirited and curious then, but Hugh knew she had since gone through a difficult year. Instead of asking if Lady Cassandra would be joining them, Hugh turned to Fournier, who paced behind the sofa.

"Has the magistrate been sent for?"

"Yes, but as he is in Swanley, we'll likely be waiting hours for his arrival," the duke replied.

"Lucky for us, a Runner has arrived."

This came from a man standing near the decanters, his flat glare locked on Hugh.

It wasn't the first condescending remark he'd been subjected to since becoming viscount. He was no fool—he knew there were those in the ton who would never accept him, title or no. Many looked down their noses at his colorful past, especially as he had been part of the working class. However, this man in particular had a larger reason for his pretentious comment.

"Lord Westbrook," Hugh said, recognizing him as one of Barty's acquaintances. The Marquess of Westbrook was about ten years Barty's senior and rumored to be as overindulgent of women and liquor as he was with the gaming tables. "As you know, I am no longer with Bow Street," Hugh said evenly. "But I will help however I can. Tell me what is known so far."

Westbrook only snorted and sipped his drink.

Fournier looked to Audrey and gestured for her to speak.

She twisted her fingers, encased in black lace gloves, before her.

"My sister and her maid are missing," she started to say, but Westbrook interrupted.

"We do not know for certain who the occupants of the coach were."

Audrey cut her eyes to him; had they been knives, they would have flayed him. "The contents of the luggage left behind will prove I am correct. Michael, I'd like to see them."

Fournier nodded and signaled a footman. "Have the trunks brought to the dowager duchess's room."

"And have her own trunks delivered back to her room," the new duchess added. She then looked to Audrey. "I insist you stay, at least for the time being."

Audrey's answering nod was wooden and distracted.

"When did you arrive at Greenbriar, Lord Westbrook?" Hugh asked.

"About an hour ago."

"And did you also come upon this abandoned coach?" Hugh continued.

"I did. My carriage passed it after the dowager duchess and her driver had already turned back for Greenbriar."

"We left a footman with the coach and the driver," Audrey put in.

"Where is the driver's body now? And the coach?" Hugh's mind easily geared back onto the well-traveled track of questioning witnesses. Being relieved from his post as Bow Street had been a significant blow; he took pride in his work and had never, not once, tired of it. Being told he could no longer do the thing he loved, and instead had to play the part of lord of the realm, had been salt in an open wound.

"The coach has been stored in the carriage house and the body is in the wine cellar for now, though we could move it to the icehouse if the need arises," Fournier replied.

"It *is* my sister's coach." With a defiant glare toward Lord Westbrook, Audrey added, "And Millie always travels with her maid."

She turned away from the marquess and met Hugh's eyes again. The subtle and quick flex of her brow said something that only Hugh was likely able to read: she knew more. Things she could not say here, in front of the others. She must have touched something on the coach, or inside it, and a vision had likely been fed to her. The extraordinary ability had helped them before with other lines of inquiry, and once he could speak to her privately, she would surely inform him.

Impatience to be alone with her warred with apprehension. The last few months had changed much in each of their lives. It seemed an impossible task to pick up where they'd left off.

"Was Lady Redding on her way to Greenbriar for the house party?"

The new duchess, Geneva, spoke up at this. "She was not on the guest list." With a quick, apologetic glance at Audrey, she added, "My husband and I are not well acquainted with the viscountess."

Knowing how Audrey felt about her sister, Hugh didn't imagine she took offense at Millie not being invited to stay at Greenbriar. But that left the question of what she had been doing near the estate.

"She lives at Reddingate in Essex, near Brentwood," Audrey supplied, still wringing her hands. "I have no idea what she could have been doing out this way."

"Could she have been coming to see you?" Hugh asked.

Audrey's pursed lips softened, and she winced. "I can't fathom why she might have been. If that was her plan, the visit was unannounced."

"Let's not forget that the coach might have been empty to begin with. Perhaps it was only transporting belongings to someplace," Westbrook said, again treating Audrey's claim as improbable.

"It was not traveling without passengers. The door was open, the steps lowered to the road," Audrey snapped, her patience thinning. As was Hugh's.

Westbrook had always been an intractable fool. That Hugh might be spending the next two weeks at Greenbriar with him made him even more reluctant to stay for the entirety of the affair. At least Thornton had accepted his own invitation, extended to him, no doubt, to give Hugh a known acquaintance. The duchess was thoughtful in that regard.

However now, with Lady Redding and her maid missing and a driver dead, Hugh had something to focus on. And Audrey, who appeared uncharacteristically uneasy, concerned him.

"I'm inclined to agree with Audrey, however, perhaps we should send a messenger to Reddingate and inquire about the driver's destination and if Lady Redding was with him." Lord Tobias's voice was as young as his nearly whisker-free cheeks.

"Yes, that makes the most sense at this point," Fournier agreed.

But Hugh shook his head. "No messenger. I will go to Reddingate myself."

Giving the servants and staff time to go through the

driver's room and his belongings or their lady's things in search of answers would not do. He also couldn't deny the allure of already leaving Greenbriar, as self-serving as it would be.

"I insist that you be shown to your room and have some refreshment before you depart," the duchess said. He wasn't above reason; he had been traveling all day and was both restless to move and famished.

He agreed to the terms and the drawing room began to empty. The duke and Tobias locked themselves into a whispered discussion, while Westbrook threw back the rest of his drink and stalked from the room.

From the corner of his vision, he saw Audrey walking stiffly toward him, as if on her way to leave as well. As she slowed in passing, her whisper was hardly audible: "Meet me in the library balcony as soon as you can."

And then, in a rustling cloud of black bombazine, she continued past him and was gone.

CHAPTER

THREE

The mezzanine in the library had become a place of refuge for Audrey over the last several weeks. Genie and Michael had been gracious hosts, giving her solitude and quiet, and for that she was thankful. However, staying with her brother- and sister-in-law also gave her an up-close view of their grief over Philip—and for that, Audrey felt only guilt. She found it easier to be alone, reading in an alcove tucked away in the mezzanine, out of view from the main library below. This last month, she had often brought her writing box with her, lining up her tools upon the alcove's desk to write to Cassie in Brighton. She would also write letters to Philip. Though they remained unsent, she would pour out her emotions on paper alone in the alcove, attempting to work through her complicated thoughts and feelings.

She was angry he left, and yet also understanding. She didn't begrudge him his chance to have the kind of freedom he'd longed for, but what about *her*? It wasn't selfish to want the same freedom, and yet as much as Philip believed his scheme would free her as well as himself, it had not. Not fully, at least. What more could he have done to free her? Offered to take her with him? Stage both of their deaths, rather than just his own? She never would have agreed, and he had known that. Still, why hadn't he at least offered it?

Out of caution, she burned her rambling letters to Philip in the grate in her room. Oddly, they helped her. Much the same way holding her brother James's nautilus shell usually did. She kept her treasured memento from her late brother stored in a compartment in the writing box. Her letters to Philip and her brother's shell would soothe her whenever she was feeling agitated.

To Audrey, the alcove was a safe spot, and it was also a perfect place to now speak with Hugh in private.

Her pulse quickened, as it seemed to have done nonstop since coming upon the coach in the road. She was worried for Millie and her maid, but her quickening pulse was not just due to concern for them. Seeing Hugh in the drawing room had somehow unsettled her *and* tempered her worry —now that he was here, she felt at ease knowing that someone competent would help her find Millie. And yet, as they had discussed the particulars of the attack on the coach, she had not been able to stave off shivers of nervousness.

She had not thought she'd see him again so soon. She hadn't been ready. He was just as handsome as ever—that hadn't changed. His rich, dark brown eyes still pierced; his strong jaw and full mouth still lent him a masculine beauty. His attire hadn't changed either, really. Perhaps he appeared a little more refined in new clothes that he had not been given to wearing as a Bow Street officer, or maybe she was only making that up in her head. Hugh had always dressed like a gentleman.

And yet, he *had* changed. How could he not have? He was a viscount now. Something about that gave Audrey the strangest sense of loss. It made no sense; she could not account for it at all. She had not lost him. Gracious, he'd never been hers to begin with! But she had still sensed a gulf between them when he'd entered the drawing room earlier. An unfamiliar, cold expanse that had made her shiver. She was grateful their first meeting occurred among several other people, and though she did not wish ill on Millie's driver or maid, or Millie herself, she was also glad that she and Hugh would have something on which to focus their attention, their conversation.

Perhaps then they would not have to discuss Philip.

How was she supposed to tell him the truth? Opening her mouth and beginning her confession seemed as daunting as scaling a mountain, its peak lost in stormy clouds. She could not even begin to think how she would say it. And if she did, wouldn't that only transfer the burden of Philip's secret onto Hugh's shoulders? Not for an instant did Audrey think he would reveal Philip's crime, for it would negatively impact her, and Hugh had proved in the past that he would go to great lengths to protect her. But how could she ask him to keep this secret?

The creak of a floorboard registered a moment before his voice cut through the muffled quiet.

"This could be a dangerous place."

Audrey spun around as he emerged from the corner of the aisle. Three such aisles cut back from the mezzanine balcony. Each aisle had a private reading alcove, complete with a chair or sofa, footstools, and a desk and lantern. Her favorite alcove provided a small round window that over-looked the lawns and the lake. But for this meeting, she'd chosen the more private, inner alcove.

She shook off her nerves with a shallow exhalation and tried to appear collected. "What is so dangerous about a library?"

He entered the alcove, the lamp Audrey had lit providing enough light for them to see by. Hugh kept his hands in his pockets, his relaxed posture only highlighting how bothered she felt in comparison. "I have no doubt that at least one debutante arriving for the house party will attempt to lure some unsuspecting eligible lord here," he replied.

Hugh's lips turned into a coy half-grin. Audrey met it, and with a shake of her head, continued with the plausible entrapment scheme. "And have a cohort stationed nearby to just...happen upon them?"

Such a thing could transpire. To be sure, it *had*. A lady's reputation could be ruined just by being found alone in such a private place with a man, and the man would then, out of honor and duty, be expected to make her an offer.

"Be wary of conniving ladies," she said, but though it was meant to be playful, the moment she said it, her stomach dropped.

One lady in particular suddenly rushed to mind: Lady Veronica Langton. The fresh-faced debutante was the daughter of the Earl of Kettleridge and just out of her second Season. She was also the woman rumored to be recently connected to Viscount Neatham.

The spike of jealousy had Audrey cutting her eyes away from Hugh. Ever since Genie had mentioned that Lord and

Lady Kettleridge had accepted the invitation, along with their daughter, Lady Veronica, Audrey had been struggling to keep her envy in check. Most times, she failed.

"I'll be on my guard," he replied lightly, but when she kept her lips sealed, he must have sensed their banter had finished. "You know something more about the incident on the road."

Good. This was firmer ground. "I held the coach's doorknob, yes, and I saw them—Millie and her maid—being taken. A man was asking about a ring, demanding Millie to hand it over."

"And did she?"

Audrey shook her head. "She said she did not have it, and she didn't appear to be lying. She was terrified, in tears of distress, I—" She stopped to draw a breath, her chest suddenly tight. "I have never seen her in such a state before."

Millie had always been coolly unaffected. Even when their father and brother died, Audrey had not seen her shed a tear. Certainly not when her husband had died, either.

Hugh moved toward the small writing desk tucked into the corner of the alcove. The high polish of the honey amber wood gleamed in the lamplight. This small space truly was the perfect spot for a tryst. And if the whispers she had heard from Cassie when she'd visited Greenbriar the previous month held any truth to them, Lady Veronica might hold designs for one with Hugh during the next fortnight.

The Neatham scandal had produced a reaction that was the total opposite of that which Audrey and Philip had endured after Philip's wrongful arrest. Instead of being delegated to the list of deplorables, the new Viscount Neatham had become an object of curiosity to both the ladies and men of the ton. His background fascinated the ladies, his former blackguard status slightly exhilarating. His handsome looks surely drew interest as well.

"You've no idea how many ladies I've overheard discussing how coarse his hands must be," Cassie had said with a roll of her eyes as she and Audrey had been playing backgammon in June. She'd lowered her voice so that Michael, reading in a chair across the room wouldn't hear. "Or how coarse he is in other ways."

Audrey had gaped at her younger sister-in-law, not so much appalled by her comment as she was by the women Cassie spoke of. Calling him coarse, treating him as if he was less than the other men of their acquaintance, and yet desiring him for such shallow reasons, had infuriated her. Ladies like the ones Cassie had overheard would certainly see Hugh as a catch for his wealth and title *now*. But they would have turned their noses up at him before.

Cassie had also related that one young lady and Hugh had been seen together at a few dinner parties in London. Cassie had not known to curb her tongue; she wasn't aware of Audrey's feelings for Hugh, or his for her. Though, as the months slipped past, their last meeting in the kitchen of his Bedford Street home—when they had both confessed to feelings that were not going to simply go away—had started to feel more and more like a hazy dream. Had things changed for Hugh? He'd said he was not in the market for a viscountess, but perhaps this Lady Veronica had appealed to him in some way...

Audrey closed her eyes and breathed deeply. This was no time to fall into the spiraling thoughts that had so recently plagued her.

"Are you unwell?" Hugh's voice reached her, and she snapped her eyes open. Concern hardened him as he inspected her, toe to crown.

"No, I'm...I'm fine. Truly. You were saying?"

"I wasn't saying anything. Neither were you." He stepped away from the desk, toward her, but then held still. "These last months must have been difficult for you. Audrey, I'm sorry. I—"

"No." She blurted it out before she could think, before she even knew she was speaking.

He frowned. "No?"

His confusion was warranted. *No* didn't make sense at all. She'd only wanted him to stop speaking. The idea of discussing Philip made her tremble, if only because she didn't want to face Hugh's wrath. He'd be furious. He'd be disappointed in her for pretending.

"I just don't wish to speak of it right now," she rushed to say, avoiding his gaze. "I'm not ready."

Hugh stepped back, to the desk, and nodded. "Of course. Forgive me."

Fresh guilt seared her. He'd done nothing wrong. But she needed to redirect the conversation. "What more would you like to know about the incident on the road?"

He cleared his throat and then, after a moment's thought, asked, "You did not see the man's face?"

"I'm afraid not, the vision was limited—it was like I was standing at the door, peering into the coach myself."

Sometimes, the scope of her visions frustrated her. There was never any telling what she would see, or how thoroughly she would see it. She could close herself off to them, too, pushing out the energy an object might transfer to her. And then other times, they caught her unaware.

She rubbed her temple. "If I were to touch something of the driver's, perhaps I could see the face of the person who shot him."

Hugh shook his head. "The cellar is being guarded by two footmen, and I can't imagine what excuse we could give for you to view the body."

She'd thought of that too. "I wish I could direct the visions. I wish I could tell you more."

Hugh shifted his position so that he faced her fully. "What you've provided is already leaps and bounds ahead of where we'd be without you. The mention of a ring gives us at least a motive for the attack."

He was right, of course, though it was a piece of information they could not share with the others, or the magistrate whenever he arrived. Nor did Audrey have any idea which ring it could be.

"Millie continued to wear her wedding band," she said, recalling the few visits she'd had with her sister since Lord Redding passed. "But I'm afraid no other jewelry of hers stood out to me."

Hugh crossed his arms and leaned his hip against the writing desk. "Take me through it. Where was the driver?"

"In the box, still seated, slumped over."

"And his weapon?"

Audrey pinned her lower lip. "I don't know. Carrigan or Travers, the footman who was with us, might recall. But the door was left open, as I told Lord Westbrook, and the steps were down."

Hugh turned his attention toward the shelves of books to

the left, his jaw tensing as he contemplated. "Highwaymen generally demand jewels and money, but it sounds as if this man—or men, if he was not acting alone—had an interest in a specific ring."

"He stopped Millie's coach, believing she had it with her?"

"If that is so, he knew where she would be traveling. He knew where and when to waylay her," Hugh replied.

On a road, far from her own home. "We need to know her planned destination," Audrey said, impatience rising. She could not sit idly and wait for the magistrate to arrive, or for Hugh to question Millie's staff. "I will go with you to Reddingate. The housekeeper might be more amenable to allowing us entry if I am with you, and there may be something there I can hold or touch that could tell us more."

Audrey expected an argument, and she received one.

"You are in mourning," Hugh pointed out.

"She is my sister. I'll care about mourning rules after we've found her."

The slow stretch of his lips happened in time with the thumping of her heart. Not very long ago, he would have grated out a complaint about her disregard for the rules. Now, he merely appeared amused.

"I know better than to try to stop you," he said with a shake of his head.

"Good. Greer and I are ready to leave when you are."

FOUR

Birds trilled within the branches of the trees lining the road. A soft breeze rustled the leaves, thick and vibrantly green now that August had come. In the narrow field running between the road and a stretch of forest, the incessant humming of beetles, crickets, grasshoppers, and flies were oddly peaceful sounds for a place where a murder and kidnapping had occurred just hours before.

Hugh paced the spot on the dusty road where Lady Redding's coach had been found. The packed dirt showed the evidence of disturbance—wheel grooves and horseshoe impressions, scuff marks, a single boot print, well preserved. But too many conveyances had since come and gone, and Hugh could not definitively say in which direction Lady Redding's abductor had driven after taking her and her maid from the coach.

The field's grasses had not been sheared and stood about hip high; tall enough to conceal a small doe, bedded down. Or a body. Ever since Hugh's driver, Norris, had pulled over at Audrey's command, and she had indicated the spot on the road, Hugh's attention had been drifting toward that field.

"Has it been searched?" he finally asked, gesturing to the meadow where dragonflies buzzed overhead. Audrey, crouching to peer closer at the boot print, stood. She looked out into the grasses.

"I don't think so." Concern dawned in her eyes. "You aren't suggesting...but they were abducted, surely?"

"Most likely. I'd like to be sure," he said. "Stay here."

"Want me to come with you, Lord Hugh?" Sir asked from where he sat in the driver's box.

"Stay there and keep watch," he called back, not wanting the boy to stumble upon anything unpleasant in the field—if, in fact, the worst was to be found there.

Hugh could practically feel the rolling of Sir's eyes and hear his light scoff. He'd ridden along with Norris as they'd left Greenbriar. Audrey and her maid, along with Hugh, had been in the carriage, their conversation stilted. Greer's presence made it impossible for them to speak freely. Though, Hugh knew it wasn't the right moment for him to say anything about the way they had parted last April.

He'd gone over it in his mind so many times that it had imprinted in his brain—peeling Audrey's glove from her hand, kissing the delicate skin of her wrist, inhaling her soft camellia scent, and admitting that he wanted her more than he'd ever wanted any woman. Also seared into his memory was the shake of his head, rejecting her when she began to suggest that they become lovers. He would not treat her as a secret, nor would he be treated as such. At the time, he hadn't known how they might overcome the obstacles standing in their path; now, a year-long mourning period was all that did.

If, of course, Audrey's feelings had not changed.

Something was wrong. Thanks to his time at Bow Street, he knew when someone was avoiding him, or keeping a secret. Audrey had shown all the signs: avoidance of eye contact, fidgeting, stiff posture. In the library's alcove, she had practically panicked when he brought up the death of the duke. It might have simply been overwhelm—her sister had just been abducted, and Audrey had again come upon a murdered individual. But he sensed it was something more.

Whatever the cause, she had been more eager to discuss what they would do to find Lady Redding. Audrey's announcement that she would be traveling with Hugh to Reddingate had not been met with understanding from the new duchess, Geneva—or Genie, as Audrey called her. The duke had also been against it, insisting that Lord Neatham had things well in hand and that Audrey should stay to speak to Sir Ridley Harrow, the magistrate, when the man arrived.

It came as no great surprise to Hugh when she dismissed their protests and smoothly said Carrigan would stay and give the report of finding the driver and abandoned coach.

It also came as no great surprise when Hugh heard her skirts swishing through the field grass behind him.

"He could have no reason to take them into the field and kill them when he could have shot Millie and her maid in the coach, as he did the driver." She was likely in denial that her sister could be dead. Hugh didn't want that to be the case. However, they had to be prepared for it.

"If he wanted a specific ring, and Millie didn't have it, he probably took her to where it was. We should go to Reddin-gate, with all haste," she went on.

"Taking her at gunpoint to her own estate where servants could intercept would be far too risky for him," Hugh explained.

Audrey reached his side. He kept his attention riveted to the grass, searching for any impressions or signs of passage. So far, there had been none.

"If he was willing to kill the driver, he must have had reason to believe Millie had the ring with her," she said. Hugh agreed.

After a few more minutes of searching, he shook his head. "Nothing. I don't see any signs of someone moving toward the trees either."

Audrey wrinkled her nose as she peered at the thick white beams, yews, and elms.

He let out a long exhalation and took off his hat. Running his fingers through his hair, the heat of the sun blazing down upon the meadow began to warm him. They stood alone, far from the ears of their party. If he wanted to bring up the late duke again, now was the time.

"I should have written to you more these last months," he said. It drew her attention from the trees, to him. The wrinkles on the bridge of her nose smoothed.

"You have been busy," she replied.

"As have you."

"Not at all," she said with a humorless laugh. "I'm not allowed to do much."

The act of mourning would certainly restrict her from most social events. It seemed to Hugh more of a form of punishment, rather than a way to honor a dead spouse.

"I know you and the late duke were close friends," he began, and even though she flinched and twisted to look at the meadow behind them, he continued, "I am sure you miss his companionship."

Audrey touched her fingers to the short black fringe of tulle that dressed the brim of her bonnet. Still, she would not look at him. "I do, but...really, we should begin toward Reddingate." She started toward the road, but Hugh caught her hand with his and halted her.

"Don't hide from me, Audrey. Please."

She held still, eyes lifting to his, then away again. He released her hand, even though Sir and Greer and Norris had likely witnessed the impropriety. "I don't want to," she whispered. "I'm sorry."

"You don't need to be sorry for anything."

As she nodded and straightened her shoulders. "Well, I am sorry," she said with a thin smile. "For drawing you away from Greenbriar almost as soon as you arrived."

He could not deny her the change of topic. Urging her to talk about Philip would only push her away. As her smile grew into something more authentic—a hint that she knew how he truly felt about the socializing about to be endured—he could only sigh.

"Ah, yes, the house party. I can't say I'm distraught to not be settling into my rooms and drinking a brandy with His Grace. I wasn't entirely looking forward to coming. Though I suppose I had to begin mixing at some point."

Audrey smoothed the front of her black skirt, then clasped her hands before her. "I was under the impression you already have been."

Hugh arched a brow. Audrey might have been tucked

away in Kent for the last few months, but that wouldn't have stopped the gossip from reaching her. He thought he knew what she was referring to. Or rather, *who*.

"I have been to a few of Sir Gabriel's dinner parties." The chief magistrate at Bow Street might have cut Hugh from his role as principal officer, but that had not stopped him from seeing the older knight. Sir Gabriel and his wife Lady Rebecca entertained at least twice a month, and now that Hugh sported a shiny new title, he'd been welcomed into their home on Tavistock Street.

He and Sir Gabriel got along well, and the magistrate had kept him informed on the goings on at Bow Street. At first, Hugh had been placed at the table near Sir Gabriel, but their dinner conversation about seedy criminals, murders, and burglaries had not met with Lady Rebecca's approval. So, Hugh had found himself further from the magistrate the next few times.

But Audrey wasn't mentioning the dinners at Tavistock Street for that reason.

She licked her lips and swished her palms over the feathered tops of some switchgrass. "I understand Lord and Lady Kettleridge were at your dinners. They will be attending Greenbriar, too, I believe?"

If there was one thing Audrey wasn't, it was subtle. Hugh bit back his amusement, even though she wasn't looking directly at him.

"Despite your number of personal investigations, you haven't improved much in your questioning tactics," he said, to which he received a sharp glare. He laughed at her expression of annoyance and culpability.

"Let me put your mind at ease," he went on, still grinning at her agitation. "I am in no danger of finding myself in one of Greenbriar's library alcoves with Lady Veronica."

It was hot in the meadow, and Audrey was already flushed, but now, her cheeks stained a deeper pink. "I suggested no such thing."

She hadn't needed to.

"I am well aware of the rumors swirling around the lady and myself," he said.

Henry Langton, the Earl of Kettleridge, had all but made it clear that his goal was to arrange a match between his beautiful and accomplished eldest daughter and Hugh. As Lord Kettleridge was good friends with Sir Gabriel, he and his wife and daughter had attended the same dinners as Hugh, and Veronica had been purposefully seated to Hugh's right or left each time.

"I hadn't heard as much," Audrey said. It was a flat out lie, though anyone not experienced in her mock innocent expressions may not have known it.

"The rumors are just that—rumor."

She shrugged. "Oh? But she is quite pretty."

"She is."

"I read that the queen called her a diamond of the first water after she made her bow."

"Indeed," he replied, his enjoyment of seeing Audrey so agitated rising. It was unkind perhaps. She had been through much since the spring, and she had warned him that mamas of the ton would begin to circle him like vultures. But surely, she remembered what he'd said—that he wasn't in the market for a viscountess.

"Are you endorsing the match, Your Grace?" Hugh

teased. Audrey spluttered and gaped, shedding her act of indifference completely.

"Goodness, no!" She gasped at her blurted answer, and now her cheeks appeared beet red rather than pink.

Hugh belted out the laughter that had been bottled up, and not even her scowling reaction could stem it.

"You should not tease me," she said, looking as cross with him as he deserved.

"Where is the fun in resisting?" he replied before curbing his humor. Or at least trying to. They had been thrust into a serious crime and potential abduction from the moment they laid eyes on each other at Greenbriar. The moment of lightheartedness had dulled the sharp edge of disorder. If only momentarily.

"Audrey, nothing has changed." He reached for her hand again, this time capturing the tips of her fingers. Their fingers laced, though lightly. They looked down at their joined hands. Then, with a clearing of her throat, she stepped back.

"There is something I must tell you." Her words rushed out, breathless. Nervous. Hugh's humor faded.

"I am listening."

"It has to do with Philip," she said, her eyes unable to meet his. She closed them, breathed in, as if bracing herself. She *had* been hiding something. Though now Hugh wasn't certain he wanted to know what it was.

"What about him?" he asked when she remained tongue tied.

"I..." She glanced over her shoulder, toward where the others waited with the carriage. "We need more privacy."

"I think you should just tell me," he said. She turned

back to him, and the panic in her eyes nearly bowled him over.

What in hell did she have to say about Philip?

A sharp whistle drew Hugh's attention to Sir, still seated on the driver's bench. The boy twisted at the hip and peered down the road, in the direction of Greenbriar.

"Riders!" he shouted to Hugh.

Audrey broke away and began to hurry toward the road, likely grateful for the reprieve. It wouldn't last. Whatever she needed to say, he would make sure it came out before the day ended.

He increased his speed, overtaking Audrey and reaching the road first. The two men approaching on horseback rode at a gallop, their tailcoats flapping behind them. It was the duke and his younger brother, Tobias.

"Michael, Tobias," Audrey said, coming out of the meadow. "What has happened?"

Their drawn expressions and heavy breathing indicated something more had gone wrong.

"We'd hoped to catch you on the road," the duke panted. "There's been news from Moorsly. Audrey, you should come with us. A woman's body has been found."

FIVE

I t was closing in on four o'clock in the afternoon when they arrived at the farm in Moorsly, a small village north of Greenbriar. Audrey had not had the occasion to visit it while she'd been staying with Michael and Genie, and as she took in the few shops and buildings in the village —a tavern and stables, an ironmonger, a grocer, a tobacconist —she could see why. There was not much offered in the way of diversions for ladies like Audrey and Genie. No milliner or dressmaker, or even a shoemaker. But the kitchen maids from Greenbriar frequently visited the grocer and farms, and that was where one such housemaid heard tell of a body that had just been pulled from the river that ran through the town.

Audrey barely said a word as Norris directed their carriage, following Michael and Tobias. Hugh tapped his foot and shifted his position incessantly as they traveled the five or so miles. She caught him glimpsing at her several times, too. What had she been thinking in that field, blurting out that she needed to tell him something about Philip? Their voices would have carried to Sir, Greer, and

Norris, especially if Hugh had started to bellow about Philip's deception. But it was as if her body needed to purge the truth. Lying to Hugh, pretending, felt unnatural. It felt more wrong than anything else had in the last few months.

Thankfully, they'd been interrupted, though the reason for it weighed on her. Michael had said that there was no word on who the woman was, but the discovery of a body on the same day as Millie's disappearance was too great a coincidence to overlook.

Time had seemed to suspend as they traveled, but upon Norris's slowing of the horses, and a small house and barn coming into view, it catapulted forward again. Her heartbeat rushed, turning her pulse rapid and her breathing uneven. She hardly noticed Hugh handing her down from the carriage, and then following him, Michael, and Tobias to where a man stood waiting by a pair of open barn doors. His white hair, wire spectacles, and the proper, if tatty, cravat suited the picture of country doctor well, and indeed, that is what he was.

"Doctor Winslow, at your service, Your Grace." The older gentleman bowed after Michael introduced himself and their party. "It is a sorry business. The young woman was taken from the Wending, just beyond Mr. Searle's turnip field. There was nothing to be done by that point. We heard there was a commotion on the road to Greenbriar? A kidnapping?"

"Yes, and a murder as well. A driver, killed," Michael replied. But Audrey's mind clung to what Doctor Winslow had imparted.

"A *young* woman, you say?"

He turned to her. "Yes, Your Grace. Could there be a connection?"

Hugh stepped forward. "If you could show us to the body?"

He still possessed the same command for respect as he had when he was working at Bow Street. The doctor jumped to it and led them into the barn. Afternoon sunlight filtered through gaps between the barn boards, gilding the dust motes floating in the air. The smell of sweet hay and pungent manure gathered in the back of her throat.

The moment she saw the canvas-tarp covered body on a plain wooden table, she knew that it wasn't Millie. The figure underneath was too petite. Millie wasn't large, but she was taller than Audrey by an inch or two and had an impressive bosom and wider hips. Relief quickly changed over to guilt; she should not have felt anything other than sorrow for the woman underneath the moth-eaten tarp, which the farmer had likely scrounged up in the barn.

"If Her Grace will prefer to remain outside?" Dr. Winslow said when he realized Audrey had followed them into the barn.

"Her Grace does not prefer," Audrey replied, then smiled. "Please, carry on. I won't perish on the spot."

With an unsettled and distinctly disapproving sniff and prop of his brow, he turned to the table. Hugh took a step closer to her as the doctor reached for the canvas. She could sense his concern, his readiness to take her arm if indeed it was Millie. But as she'd already suspected, when the canvas was drawn back, the face of a woman she had never met was revealed.

She was indeed young, likely no more than twenty.

Graciously, her eye lids had been closed, though they appeared bruised by the ashy blue tinge of death. Her lips were bone white, her dress and hair still damp. The cut, style, and quality of her dress would have informed the others of this woman's status, but it was Audrey's earlier vision that confirmed the poor woman's identity.

"Millie's maid," she said, her throat tight. She had been alive in the vision, wide eyed with confusion and fright, and now...here she lay, dead.

My god. The kidnapper had killed this maid. What had become of Millie?

Now, Audrey was grateful for Hugh's nearness. She turned away from the body and toward him as he gently gripped her elbow.

"Are you certain?" Michael asked. She nodded.

"Do you know her name?" the doctor asked next.

"No." Audrey drew a deep breath. "I...recall her. But I don't know her name."

That answer wasn't a complete fabrication.

"Did she drown?" Tobias asked, but Hugh must have seen the blood on the bodice of her gown at the same moment as Audrey.

"No," Hugh said, his fingers brushing the stain. The blood had spread through the cloth, helped along by the soaking of her gown in the river.

"I have only done a preliminary examination, but it appears she was shot," Dr. Winslow said. His white brows pulled together with an expression of sorrow.

Audrey's stomach lurched. The violence of it, the senselessness, made her ill. This maid had people who loved her, and now they would suffer from the loss of her.

At her neckline was a simple lace ribbon, onto which a small silver cross had been fixed. Audrey nibbled her lower lip. Silver was a reliable metal when it came to reading memories.

"The viscount and I are on our way to Reddingate," she said. "I will take this necklace with me to show the servants there. They will be able to confirm it is the maid and name her."

Hugh undoubtedly knew what she was about when he stepped forward and began to untie the ribbon from around the woman's neck. He caught her eye, a bit of mischief in his rich mahogany irises, when he handed her the necklace. With her gloves protecting her skin, whatever the small cross had to tell her stayed firmly locked within the silver. She dropped it into her pocket, eager to be gone from the musty, humid barn.

Doctor Winslow assured them that he would place the woman's body into the town's mausoleum for now, until it could be identified properly and claimed. As they left the barn, Audrey dragged in a deep breath, grateful for the ability to do so. Saddened that the maid could not. And terrified at the possibility that Millie, too, had been killed. And all over *a ring*?

"Tobias and I will return to Greenbriar to greet the magistrate and inform him of this," Michael said. He peered up at the sky, which was turning golden as the afternoon waned. "You will reach Reddingate well past nightfall. Perhaps you should delay until tomorrow."

"No, we must go tonight," Audrey said, impatient. Besides, sleep would elude her if she spent it at Greenbriar waiting for dawn.

"We will be fine," Hugh agreed. "I'll ride in the box with Norris."

Michael grimaced but didn't argue. He mounted his horse, as did Tobias, and they rode back in the direction of the main road.

Unlike Audrey, Greer had chosen to remain outside the barn, waiting with Hugh's driver and Sir. She came to attention as Audrey approached, a question in her eyes. Audrey shook her head. "It isn't my sister."

"The maid?" Greer asked. In a flash of unbidden wretchedness, Audrey pictured Greer laid out on that table, under the tarp, instead of Millie's maid. It nearly drew all the breath from Audrey's lungs.

She gave a short nod, and Greer's lips tensed. Norris handed them into the carriage, and this time, Sir climbed in with them. The chassis rocked as Hugh joined his driver, and then, they were rolling away from Moorsly.

Greer folded her hands in her lap and took a cautious glimpse toward Audrey. "I am certain Lady Redding will be unharmed. Surely the kidnapper will demand a ransom for her safe return?"

It was a possibility, but with the memory of the man demanding Millie hand over "the ring" she didn't quite believe it was a situation in which a ransom would suffice. The idea that the driver and maid had been expendable, while Millie was not, lit a fire in her chest.

Audrey allowed a few minutes to pass in silence, until Greer had turned to look out the window and Sir had slouched, resting the back of his head on the squabs. There was only one way to know what the maid's last moments had entailed, and if she had been with Millie at the time. She peeled off her glove, a relief in the humid weather, and with damp palms, reached into her skirt's pocket. Without taking the necklace out, she closed her palm and fingers around the silver cross pendant.

She bit back a gasp as the first images barreled into her mind, erasing her view of the carriage interior almost completely. The visions weren't always this potent; they were sometimes weak, like watercolors bleeding across the fibers of a paper. The strong ones were solid, almost as if Audrey could reach out and touch them. This one exploded before her eyes, vibrant and close. It was also loud, nothing like the muffled, underwater sound of most visions.

Almost instantly, Audrey saw a woodland, the trees tall and thin. Ferns blanketed the ground. The world shook—the maid was running. She threw quick glances over her shoulder, and behind her, coming through the trees and ferns, was a man's figure.

Facing forward again, the maid was nearing a field. Tall grass. A sloping hill. The images were scattered and chaotic, and then there was water—the banks of a swollen river. Audrey knew what happened from there, and with no wish to see it, and no sign of Millie in the field or nearby, Audrey gathered a breath and pushed back, deeper into the stored memories. The further back she looked, the dimmer the memories would appear. They would soon turn murky and opaque and then fade to nothing at all.

Where was Millie?

There.

As Audrey allowed the memories to surface again in her mind, Millie was standing before her. Tears streaked her red cheeks, her hair, normally coiffed to perfection, loose from its pins. Her face screwed up, as if in anguish.

"You betrayed me?" she said to the maid, the sound of her voice muffled as the energy leeched from the silver pendant. "How could you betray me?"

Audrey clung to the moment, clung to the memory, needing to hear more. To know more. But as with every object, the energy, and the vision it gave her, depleted. The interior of the carriage returned, the golden sunset light shedding over a sleeping—and snoring—Sir. Greer was still peering out the window, lost in thought, oblivious to the short trip Audrey's mind had just taken.

It seemed Millie's maid had betrayed her.

And perhaps that is what had gotten her killed.

SIX

T he lights of Reddingate erased the knot of worry that had started to grip Audrey as their carriage traveled along the rapidly darkening roads. Rather than confidence at Hugh sitting with Norris, on alert for anything suspicious, Audrey had only felt fear. Millie's driver had been killed; if Hugh were to come to any harm...well, she could barely stand to think of it. He had his flintlock to be sure, but not understanding, not knowing the reason for Millie's kidnapping, or what in the world she'd been doing so close to Greenbriar, made Audrey wonder if any of this might have something to do with her, too. What ring? There were no family heirlooms from their mother or uncle that Audrey knew of.

The few hours ride to Reddingate had been quiet in Hugh's carriage, with Greer drifting to sleep a few times, and Sir, shifting restlessly on the bench across from her. The boy's scrubbed and neat appearance with his tailored livery and shiny boots, had startled Audrey at first. Things truly *had* changed. But then his scowl, his distrusting stare, had settled more familiarly. Of course, Hugh would have kept Sir on and made him a part of his new life as viscount.

Audrey had attempted to engage the boy in conversation shortly after seeing the images the necklace had shown her, when the wheels had hit a bump in the road and Sir had snorted awake. She'd asked how he was finding his new position. He'd tensed his shoulders and muttered a polite reply before looking out the window.

"Is there something wrong, Sir?" It wasn't like him to be so concise or use such proper English.

The boy sneaked a look at her. "I ain't supposed to talk much to the toffs, now I'm Lord Hugh's assistant and all."

She bit back a grin. "Who told you that?" Surely, not Hugh.

"Baz."

"Since when do you obey Basil?"

Sir frowned and said nothing, but she could see him thinking about the question.

"Sir, I hope I am not just some toff. You can speak freely to me."

The boy's shoulders had dropped, and he crossed his arms over his chest, sitting back against the squabs. "Then I can tell ya that the new duke acts like he's got a tall stick up his arse?"

The grin she'd been biting back forced its way over her lips. A glimpse toward Greer showed she was still dozing, thank goodness. "The new duke is dealing with two murders and a missing lady. I think he is entitled to being a little tense." Sir began to hunch and scowl. "However, don't tell anyone, but...he *can* be rather severe."

At that, Sir had smirked with pleasure. Now, as they

reached the front drive to Reddingate, his tricorne was in place and he'd positioned himself at the door, ready to open it for her and Greer.

"I'm so hungry my gut's starting to eat itself," Sir muttered.

Greer glared, but before she could admonish him, the carriage came to a stop and shook as Norris and Hugh descended. Sir opened the door, and Audrey saw a greeting party crowding Reddingate's entrance. Footmen holding lanterns approached their after-dark guests with courteous curiosity.

As Norris and Sir saw Audrey and Greer to the ground, Hugh addressed the butler who next emerged from the home, the windows of which were not fully lit. With no mistress at home, there would be no need to have the rooms ready.

After introducing himself to the butler, Grimes, Hugh stated they had pertinent information on the viscountess, and they were swept inside, into Millie's receiving room. Audrey's eyes traveled around it. She had not been at Reddingate in at least a dozen years. Not since Millie had borne her first child, a boy, Steven. He would be around thirteen now, likely at Eton or Harrow. Audrey did not know him; she wouldn't be able to identify him in a crowd. The disconnect between herself and her sister was that thorough.

And yet, it was a possibility that Millie had been coming to see her.

While the housekeeper, Mrs. Larson asked a few maids to bring tea and prepare meals and rooms for their guests, Hugh stepped to Audrey's side and whispered, "The necklace?"

She held his inquisitive gaze as Greer and Sir followed the

maids from the receiving room. "As soon as we are alone," she replied softly.

Hugh turned to Grimes and Mrs. Larson. Briefly, he reported the events of the day. The two head servants exchanged looks of utter shock before Mrs. Larson clapped her hands over her mouth and sought the nearest chair. A footman dashed away, ostensibly to inform the rest of the house.

"I cannot account for it." Grimes blinked and shook his head as Mrs. Larson attempted to regain her composure. "Her ladyship was to visit Lady Edgerton at Haverfield. Sammy made no mention of first going to Kent."

He rubbed at his creased forehead, his gaze drifting toward the parquet floor as overwhelm stole his attention.

"Sammy is the driver?" Hugh asked. Grimes nodded.

"Good man. He was a new hire. Only been here a month."

Audrey took the pendant from her pocket and held it for Grimes and Mrs. Larson to see. "This was worn by the young woman pulled from the river. Can you confirm it belonged to Lady Redding's maid?"

Mrs. Larson stood and, visibly bracing herself, approached Audrey's outstretched hand. She shuddered and took a kerchief from her pocket. Pressing it to the tip of her nose, she nodded. "Celine Woods, Your Grace."

Celine. Attaching a name to the body she'd viewed gave the poor woman another layer of depth. What had she done to betray her mistress?

"How long has she been lady's maid here?" she asked instead.

"Four and a half years," Mrs. Larson answered with a

certain dip of her head. "She came on just after his lordship passed. Her ladyship had never been fond of her first maid. Enid had been maid to his lordship's first wife, and he had refused to let her go."

So, once her husband died, Millie had hired Celine.

"Miss Woods was devoted to her ladyship," Mrs. Larson continued, sniffling again. "She was raised in Kinsdale, just down the road. Proud to be a viscountess's attendant."

It was a coveted position, indeed. And yet, Millie had accused Celine of betrayal in her last moments.

"Does Miss Woods have family in Kinsdale?" Hugh asked. The housekeeper seemed to wilt.

"A father. Poor man. He's not well. He'll be crushed." Her hand trembled as she again touched the kerchief to her nose.

"I will visit him tomorrow," Grimes said somberly. Audrey did not envy his task of informing Mr. Woods.

"What was the purpose for Lady Redding's visit to Haverfield?" Hugh asked.

"She didn't say," Mrs. Larson replied. "Though I do recall being surprised by the announcement that she was visiting again. She had just been at Haverfield last month."

"I believe it might have had something to do with a letter she received," Grimes said.

A stutter of interest slowed, then quickened, Audrey's heartbeat. She looked to Hugh, who was already glancing at her.

"When was this letter delivered?" Hugh asked.

"A week ago, I'd say."

"And only then did she decide upon a visit to Hertfordshire?"

Grimes nodded. Then, after a thoughtful frown, said, "It did seem to excite her. The letter, I mean."

"Excite how?" Hugh asked just as Audrey asked, "Do you know who sent it?"

Grimes replied to Audrey's question first. "I do not know the sender," he said, then replied to Hugh. "Her ladyship suffers from episodes of nerves, but this was something altogether different. I would venture to say she was both pleased *and* concerned."

Mrs. Larson bobbed her head and patted her skirt pocket. "Oh, yes, I always keep my smelling salts ready for her nervous fits, and just yesterday, she required them."

That her sister had suffered from fainting spells and nervousness was not overly remarkable. Millie had always been a bit rigid and jittery, easy to upset and prone to overreact.

After her husband's death, Audrey had expected Millie to marry again. She was a wealthy viscountess, and though she had four children under the age of thirteen, there were plenty of peers who would benefit greatly from pairing Lord Redding's wealth with their own. But Millie had not remarried.

Four years ago, when she was newly widowed and entering half-mourning, Audrey had been engaged to marry Lord Bainbury. When Philip had swooped in and stolen her away from the earl, Millie had been indignant. Bitterly, their mother explained to Audrey that she had hoped for the Duke of Fournier to consider her. For a time, Audrey had thought Millie was avoiding her for that reason—however irrational Millie's envy had been. Surely there had been offers since then? And yet, she had still not remarried. Estranged as she had been from her sister for so long, Audrey had never troubled herself to ponder why.

"Can you think of anyone who would wish Lady Redding any harm?" Hugh asked. "Anyone she quarreled with lately? Any servants she'd put out?"

They shook their heads, clearly flummoxed.

"Where are my nieces and nephews?" Audrey asked, recalling the darkened upstairs windows.

"The children stay with Mr. and Mrs. Stanwyck for most of the summer, near Brighton. They are great friends of her ladyship and have several children, you see," Mrs. Larson replied, a glint of pleasure lifting her drawn features. Mrs. Stanwyck, Jane, was Millie's stepdaughter—Lord Redding's only living child from his first marriage. Millie and her stepdaughter were just about the same age, and from what Audrey had gleaned even from a distance, they liked each other immensely.

"I would like to see her rooms," Hugh said. "As well as the rooms where Sammy and Miss Woods resided." At the affronted looks of alarm he received, he explained, "Previous to being viscount, I was a Bow Street officer." Only slightly appeased by that, Hugh continued with a bald-faced lie. "I am assisting the magistrate in this matter, and if I can see this letter you mentioned, it might tell us where her ladyship has been taken."

He sounded convincing, and indeed, Millie's two head servants assented, leaving Audrey and Hugh in the receiving room in order to have the fire in Millie's bedchamber stoked, the lamps lit. They had not been gone a full breath when Hugh faced Audrey. "Tell me."

The cross pendant was still clutched in her palm. As she

set it on a small round table near the sofa, she divulged what she'd seen. Hugh stood close, so that she didn't have to speak very loud for him to hear.

"Celine betrayed Millie," she whispered. "I don't know how, just that she did, and Millie appeared shocked and devastated to learn of it."

"No mention of a ring?"

She shook her head. "Or of a letter. Celine must have gotten away from the kidnapper somehow. She was running out of the woods and into a field by a river when..." Audrey stopped. She had purposefully pushed away from that part of the vision, not wanting to see it or experience it through Celine's eyes.

Aware of what she meant to say, Hugh brushed his fingers down her arm, then gently gripped her elbow. He stood close; too close to be proper. The clicking of shoes neared the door and he stepped away just before Mrs. Larson reappeared.

"If you'll follow me," the older woman said, and she led them from the receiving room to the stairs, up to the first floor of the home.

Reddingate was about the same size as Haverfield, but in Tudor style with gables and slopes, lending it a medieval look. The style was refined, if a bit aged, and Audrey sensed the décor had not been updated for quite some time. It surprised her, as the dark wood and heavy furnishings and wine red carpets did not seem in Millie's taste at all. Then again, what did she know of her sister? Nothing much, she realized.

Her bedchamber smelled of rose oil. The silver-gray silk paper on the walls reflected lamplight and the new fire, building in the hearth grate. Mrs. Larson stood aside as Audrey went to her sister's side table and opened the slim drawer; it was empty. Utterly bare. It was suspicious, though Audrey could not articulate why even in her own mind.

The housekeeper watched them as Hugh opened a few drawers on a short bureau and gently pushed aside the items they held. Audrey moved to a small writing desk near a window, feeling Mrs. Larson's watchful stare on her back. The woman was only making sure her mistress's belongings were treated well; she might have also been hesitant to leave a man and woman alone in a bedchamber.

When Audrey opened the writing desk's main drawer and reached inside, her knuckles collided with a small nub of metal. She flipped her hand and felt the metal—a latch. She coughed loudly to clear her throat as she pulled the latch, and sure enough, she heard a soft, telling click underneath her coughing. A hidden compartment.

Audrey kept coughing, her throat becoming raw as she turned to Mrs. Larson.

"Could I bother you for a glass of water, Mrs. Larson? I know tea is being prepared, but I don't think..." she trailed off with another false cough, her eyes welling with tears at the effort to sound authentic.

"Oh, yes, Your Grace, the tea, forgive me. I think Hannah must have brought it to the receiving room." She started through the open door, but then paused, clearly torn between standing her post and accommodating a dowager duchess.

"Water would do just fine, Mrs. Larson, thank you," she said, clearing her throat again. She dropped into the desk's chair and fanned herself with her hand; that pushed Mrs.

Larson into a decision. She swept from the room, and knowing she would not be away for long, Audrey immediately hinged at the hips and peered under the writing desk.

"You are a terrible actress," Hugh said as he came to the desk. Audrey cut him a glare as she reached for the small shelf under the desk that the latch had released.

"Then you will be relieved to know I have no designs on shirking society completely and joining the theater." The reply elicited a roll of his eyes and a snort of laughter. Her fingers touched a stack of papers, and she drew them out.

"A hidden compartment," she said, bringing a bundle of papers, bound together in ribbon, into view. They were letters, all folded with their emerald-green wax seals broken.

"They look to be all from the same person," Hugh said.

Audrey set the stack on the desk and pulled the silken ribbon's knot. She lifted the top letter and opened it. Hugh took the next one from the stack. They had all been sealed with the same green wax, a letter C pressed into the seal. As they were limited to a minute at the most before the house-keeper returned, Audrey could only skim the letter. From the greeting, she knew the nature of it.

"*My dearest Millie,*" Hugh read from his aloud. Audrey's read: *My darling Millie.*

"They are love letters," Audrey said, her astonishment growing. Millie had been hiding them, even from her maid. Was this how Miss Woods had betrayed her? At the bottom of the page, the man had signed his name. "Reggie. No surname."

"He would have no call to sign it, if they were already on intimate terms," Hugh said. Then, still reading, "He speaks of living in India. Exports of fabric. Cotton, muslin, silk..."

Audrey quickly read the first lines of the letter in her hand. "Odd. He says he is in London in this letter. And that he'll be at Haverfield on August the sixteenth. He asks to meet her there and wants to know if she still has it. *It?*"

"The sixteenth is tomorrow," Hugh said.

Audrey peered at the date etched at the top of the page. "This was written a little over a week ago. It must be the same letter Grimes mentioned. The one that excited Millie."

She held her breath as she set the paper down to remove her gloves. Hugh lowered the letter in his hand. "Audrey. Maybe you shouldn't—"

She ignored him and his worry and gripped the paper again, closing her eyes and opening her mind. But as usual, paper was notoriously weak when it came to retaining energy and transmitting visions. All that cropped up in her mind was the foggiest image of Millie reading the letter. And then it was gone again.

Sighing heavily, she set the paper back onto the stack. "Nothing. But if she was supposed to meet this Reggie fellow, he might have something to do with her disappearance."

She puzzled over what the 'it' was that he referred to in the letter. Was Millie supposed to have something of his?

Hugh frowned, setting down the letter he held and picking up another one. "They were to meet at Haverfield tomorrow, not Greenbriar today. So why did she direct her driver for Kent?"

"To fetch the 'it' his letter mentioned?" An idea cropped up. "The ring, perhaps?"

"Possibly. We shouldn't speculate just yet, not with so little information to go on."

Audrey narrowed her eyes at him, annoyed, even though he had the right of it. Not that she would admit as much.

Hugh held the letter he was skimming aloft. "Cartwright. He writes here that he has been waiting for what feels like a lifetime to call her *Lady Cartwright*."

"Reggie Cartwright. Reginald, presumably. Have you heard of a Lord Cartwright?"

The creaking of floorboards on the landing outside the bedchamber alerted them to the housekeeper's return. Audrey quickly gathered the pile of letters and stuffed them into the pocket of her skirt, grateful she had them sewn into all her skirts, even if they were unfashionable. It would have taken twice as long to open her reticule and deposit them in there.

Hugh lowered his voice, met her eyes, and said, "Keep your lamp lit. I will find you tonight," a mere second before Mrs. Larson swept back into the room, breathless, and with a pitcher of water and a glass, already filled.

Audrey sipped it, her ears burning, and not just with her poor acting. Hugh's promise should not have excited her as much as it did. But they needed to go over the letters together, in private, didn't they? Without the housekeeper looking on. For if Millie hid these letters, she was surely hiding the man's interest from her staff. Why? Who was he if he had been in India? And what sort of trouble had he brought back with him?

SEVEN

Hugh paced his guest room until just after midnight, then decided it was time.

Opening the door, he sighed in relief to find the landing empty. Audrey had heeded his instruction and kept her lamps lit; from the base of her guest room's door, dim light flooded the carpet. Earlier, after Hugh and Audrey had searched the driver's and maid's rooms and found nothing of note, they'd been shown to their respective rooms. A light meal had been delivered, but Hugh had barely taken a bite as he'd waited for the house to quiet.

Now, he rapped a soft knock upon her door. Being caught trying to enter a lady's bedchamber would certainly reflect poorly on them both, and if Grimes and Mrs. Larson were vigilant, they would be sending a footman every now and again to check on the upstairs landing.

Hugh had contemplated waiting until morning to speak to Audrey about the letters, but he had another reason for insisting on a private meeting that night.

I have something to tell you, she'd said earlier. *It's about Philip.*

Whatever it was, Hugh suspected he wasn't going to like it.

The door opened an inch, and then all the way as Audrey hauled him inside. She wore her hair in a single plait and a blue silk banyan over her nightgown. Greer had brought along a small bag, to provide a change of clothes and her night things. He breathed in the camellia soap she had washed with.

"We must go to Haverfield," she whispered as soon as the door clicked shut behind her. "I've read the letters. They were in love, Millie and Lord Cartwright. Of course, we only have his letters to go by, but the way he worded them made it sound as though Millie reciprocated his feelings."

Hugh nodded. He'd already worked it out for himself that they would have to pay Hertfordshire a visit. Thankfully, Haverfield was in the southern part of the county.

"You think Lord Cartwright will be there, waiting for her?"

She nodded, then tugged the banyan tighter around her. It had not slipped, but she suddenly seemed uncomfortable. Perhaps for good reason. The last time he'd been alone with her in a bedchamber, her own at Violet House, he'd nearly taken her to bed. She'd all but asked him to. The only thing stopping him had been his refusal to share Audrey with the duke, even if she and the duke were not lovers but chaste friends.

Now, that obstacle had been erased. And he felt like the worst piece of shite for being happy about it. But after her odd comment in the field that afternoon, he knew he could not rest until she told him what she'd meant to say.

"Earlier, you said you had something to tell me."

Audrey stiffened, her fingers picking at the silk sleeve of her robe. She licked her lips and nodded. "You're going to be angry with me."

Hugh frowned. He'd been angry with her before, to be sure. Hesitation stole over him; she'd paled a little. Whatever it was she had to say, she was truly worried.

He stepped forward but didn't reach for her arms, the way he longed to. Something told him she would only flinch away. "Let me decide about that."

A breath juddered in her throat, and she closed her eyes. As if she couldn't bear to look at him. Fear that she was about to confess that she no longer held feelings for him sliced deep. But then, what she did say cut far deeper.

"Philip..." She paused, then started again. "Philip didn't die. He wants everyone to believe he did, but the truth is, he didn't drown. He has simply left."

The room swallowed her confession. In the silence that followed, Hugh couldn't breathe. Couldn't speak. For several moments, he questioned if he'd heard her correctly. Or if he had, in fact, fallen asleep in his room and this was not reality, but a nightmare.

Slowly, Audrey's lashes parted, and when she saw Hugh standing there, statuesque, she blinked. "Say something."

Barely leashed fury clipped his words. "Where is he?"

She shook her head. "I don't know. He refused to say where he was going, but...he said I will not hear from him again. Ever."

Her voice quavered over those words. The enormity of

her confession smacked him then. It turned him inside out, and yet Hugh could only grate out a huff of mirthless laughter.

"I should have known." He stalked away, toward a window, still chewing on bitter laughter.

Audrey followed. "Why should you have?"

"Because it was too easy," Hugh replied, his back still turned to her. The knot in his stomach expanded. "Because he's a self-absorbed bastard who once again does as he pleases and leaves you to pick up the pieces."

Audrey made a noise to hush him—his voice had deepened, and risen, with anger. He spun around, arms held out at his side. "You wish me to be quiet, to keep the truth to myself? My god, Audrey, the man has let the world believe he is dead. His own brothers, his sister. What's worse, he's charged you with keeping up the ruse. He's used you unspeakably, and you want me to *hush*?"

With a pulse of panic, she looked to the bedroom door and then back to him. "That isn't true! If I had demanded he stay, that he abandon his plan, I know he would have."

Hugh sucked in a breath as if she'd pummeled him in the gut. "You consented to this?"

"No, of course not. I tried everything I could think of to dissuade him, but once he's set his mind to something, it's like redirecting the tide. If I forced him to stay, he would have been miserable. And I would have been miserable seeing him that way. For all his faults, I love him. I want him to be happy—"

"And what about you? What do you deserve? Less than he does, apparently."

Hugh scrubbed a hand over his jaw, cutting off the rest of

his resentful words. He'd spent the last months feeling guilty as hell for allowing the barest sense of hope now that the duke was gone. He'd gone so far as to consider what would happen after her mourning ended. That she would be free for him to offer his hand. That she would accept him.

Now, he didn't know what to think. Except that she was still *bloody married*.

He exhaled, his throat tight. "It's been a long and trying day. We both need sleep," he said flatly and started for her door.

"Hugh, no, please." She caught his arm as he passed. "I never wanted to lie—I couldn't, not to you. I never wanted this—"

He covered her hand with his, then gently lifted it from the crook of his arm. He turned it and pressed his lips to her knuckles. Eyes closed, he breathed in the light floral scent of her skin. Then, before he could say anything else to wound her, he released her and stepped back.

"Rest. We'll discuss this another time. We leave for Haverfield first thing in the morning."

Then, without meeting her eyes, which he suspected were glassy with tears and disappointment, he turned and left.

———

Morning haze still hovered over the lawns of Reddingate, dew glistening on the blades of grass, when Hugh and Audrey departed the next day. He'd directed Norris and Sir to return to Greenbriar and deliver the identities of the dead maid and driver to Fournier and the magistrate. Thornton would have arrived for the house party by then, and Sir was to ask him what he knew about Lord Cartwright. Grant Thornton was a fount of information about the ton; he had a mind like a steel trap, and the company he kept—a mix of ton and demimonde—provided him with more gossip than what Hugh had been privy to the last six years as a Bow Street officer.

Meanwhile, Hugh, Audrey, and Greer would travel to where Millie and Cartwright had planned to meet —Haverfield.

The burden of having to present herself to her mother and uncle had been plainly visible when he'd met with Audrey in the breakfast room at Reddingate. Either that, or the burden stemmed from their tense argument and parting the night before. Hugh hadn't slept at all. He'd lain in bed, stewing with visions of hunting Philip down wherever he was hiding on the Continent and thrashing him to within an inch of his life. Hugh had floundered for some sort of foothold until dawn, trying to decide where he and Audrey could possibly go from here. The law said she was a widow. The truth said otherwise.

What if he came back? Someday, he may wish to resume the life he'd given up and left behind. Where would that leave Audrey if she had dared to move on by then? Where would that leave *Hugh*?

She was quiet as they rode in a phaeton, borrowed from Reddingate's stables toward her childhood home. Hugh was at the reins, with Greer seated between them. He was some-what grateful he would not feel Audrey's leg and hip brushing against his for the length of the drive, but the maid's presence also banished any possibility of a frank discussion.

It was probably for the best.

Barbs of irritation grew under his skin the closer they became to Haverfield. Audrey despised her mother and uncle, and her childhood had not been a happy one. It was going to be damn hard to not punch the baron square in the nose for sending Audrey away to Shadewell Sanatorium, an asylum in Northumberland. But if they wanted answers about Millie and Lord Cartwright, he would have to restrain himself.

Three hours of road travel in the open phaeton, with the sun and humidity and dust, left them looking and feeling weary as they reached Haverfield's drive. It was a somber procession up to the main manor, a Grand Baroque home with fine prospects of the surrounding dales.

Hugh helped Greer down to the crushed stone drive, then Audrey. He held her hand for an extra moment and tensed his fingers around hers.

"I'm well, I promise," she said to him.

He'd seen her like this before, when she'd been preparing to enter Shadewell for the first time since her release. She had forced back her distress and gathered her mettle, wearing it around her shoulders like a protective cloak.

"And I will do everything in my power to keep my fists to myself," he said as they approached the front door. A pang of victory filled his chest when the ice of her protective shield melted long enough for her to chuff soft laughter.

As Audrey was known here, the footman allowed them into the front hall and the butler greeted them. However, when Audrey's mother joined them in the drawing room, the baroness's cantankerous expression wasn't warranted in the least.

"I wasn't aware you were in Hertfordshire," she said sharply before settling herself into a chair. "Nor did you send word that you planned to visit. I should have been more prepared had you thought to do so."

Audrey, who had lowered herself to perch upon the edge of a chair, ignored her mother's rude greeting.

"Is Millie expected at Haverfield today?" she asked, not mincing a single word.

The baroness startled. Though she was still handsome for her age, her grimace of annoyance was as ugly an expression as Hugh had ever seen.

"What? Today? No. Why, what is this about?"

"Lady Redding left her home yesterday morning, telling her staff that she was coming here," Hugh said, noting that the baroness had not so much as looked his way. She jutted her chin and took a deep breath, prolonging her stare straight ahead, at her daughter rather than at him.

"I have no notion as to why she would do such a thing. She already visited me last month for a fortnight."

"I did not realize we were expecting guests." Lord Edgerton entered the room, his baleful glare lingering on Hugh, where he stood next to Audrey's chair. It then shifted to his niece. "Your Grace," he greeted her, treating the title like a piece of gristle caught in his teeth. Then, without looking at Hugh directly, "Lord Neatham. Why have the pair of you descended upon Haverfield this time?"

The last had been a year ago, when Lady Bainbury had been killed in the Fournier Downs parkland, and a Haverfield kitchen maid had met with the same fate. Their deaths had been at the hand of another Haverfield maid. That they had been connected to a murder scandal had surely inconvenienced the baron and Lady Edgerton. Selfish snobs, the pair of them.

"Do you know a man by the name of Lord Reginald Cartwright?" Hugh asked.

He had learned to pay attention to physical reactions whenever he questioned people during an inquiry. There were always small tells to indicate whether they planned to deflect the question, lie, or freeze with indecision. The stiffening of the baron's posture, the slowing of his gait as he cut a path to the baroness's side, gave Hugh his answer: The name meant something to Edgerton.

"Why do you ask?" the baron said.

It was to be deflection, then. Hugh swallowed his impatience. "If you will answer the question."

The baron sneered. "May I remind you, *Neatham*, that you are no longer a Runner. Bow Street ousted you."

The emphasis placed on his title crystalized his derision. The baron had been friendly with Barty and no doubt held Hugh in contempt for his ruination.

"And may I remind you, Edgerton, that I now outrank you. Answer the question."

The scowl etching itself into the man's face and twisting his lips was almost as satisfying as breaking his nose would have been. For several long moments, the baron grappled with his pride and anger, and the dowager baroness bristled on his behalf.

Not quite dowager, though, was she? Edgerton had never married after inheriting his late brother's title, and so another woman had not claimed the title of baroness. Instead, the two of them lived together outside marriage. While marrying her dead husband's brother would have been theoretically valid, it was highly frowned upon by ecclesiastical law and easily voidable if the marriage was challenged by anyone. And it was rumored Edgerton had a cousin in line to inherit who would readily do so. It also would be rife with scandal. That was something the two of them avoided at all costs. So instead, they lived here, in Hertfordshire, year-round. Far from the probing eyes of London society.

The baron, practically fulminating, replied, "Yes, I knew Cartwright."

"When were you acquainted?"

Edgerton turned on his heel and made his way to a side-board of decanters. "When Millie was just out. Cartwright wanted to marry her."

"You refused the match?" Audrey's surprise lifted her voice to a breathy pitch.

"Without question!" her mother chimed in. "We could not allow her to marry someone of his..." She creased her forehead as she thought of the next word. "Circumstance."

"What circumstance would that be?" Hugh asked.

"The man is half Indian," Edgerton barked as he finished pouring himself a brandy. "The Marquess of Montague's heir was with the East India Company, and he fell in with some provincial princess or some such; there are countless numbers of them there, I am told. Married her, against Montague's wishes. Then the pair of them went off and died of some fever."

The barbs under Hugh's skin began to lengthen and sharpen. The baron was an odious man, speaking as though Montague's son and wife had elected to die.

"And I presume they had a child. Cartwright," Hugh said.

"Yes. And he turned out very pigmented indeed," the baroness said with a sigh and shake of her head.

Audrey made a noise in her throat before standing from her chair. She caught Hugh's eye, her exasperation high. The blatant distaste the baron and baroness felt for Lord Cartwright's skin color clearly appalled her, as it did Hugh.

"You refused the match based on skin pigmentation?" Audrey asked.

"Not just that. The boy had no proper respect for his own position," Edgerton snapped. "Montague is to blame. He brought the orphan to England and put him through school in France—at great expense. Gave the boy airs. Ambition."

Hugh gritted his molars. "He *is* heir to a marquessate."

"Lord Redding was far more suitable for Millie," the baroness said.

No doubt because of his skin color. Hugh would have thought money and titles would be of primary importance to the likes of Edgerton and Audrey's mother. But it appeared their depths of character were even shallower than he'd first discerned.

Audrey stopped before a small oil portrait of a young woman, framed in gold filigree. Three paintings had been framed and set upon the table. Audrey's had been obscured and set behind a vase, but Millie's and that of a young man were on more prominent display.

Hugh observed that Millie had dark hair, closer to brown than Audrey's gold. Her squared jaw lent her a bold appearance, her straight nose and thin brows sharpening it.

Audrey's portrait accurately depicted her own heart-shaped jawline and soft lips, her upturned nose, and perceptive eyes, so Hugh presumed Millie's was a fair representation of her. The third portrait was older, from a different artist, and he presumed it to be of James, Audrey's late brother. He had Millie's bold jaw, but Audrey's upturned nose.

"Why did I not know anything about Lord Cartwright?" Audrey asked.

"Why should you have?" her mother replied, impatiently. "You were a child. No more than eight or nine. It was none of your concern."

The callousness shown toward Audrey made Hugh want to set the whole of Haverfield afire and burn it to the ground. His own mother had rejected him, but she'd at least given him the chance to be loved by another woman, one who'd longed to be a mother. Lady Edgerton had never made an effort. He bit his tongue against words of anger and instead kept his focus on questions that needed answers.

"Did your daughter keep in contact with him?"

The baroness sent him a scathing glare. "Don't be absurd, of course she did not."

"But did she love Lord Cartwright?" Audrey asked.

At this, her mother scoffed and turned her eyes toward the ceiling. "She knew her duty and did not cause any fuss. Millie, for one, was grateful for all we did for her."

The bastions holding back his temper threatened to breach, but Audrey was fast to intercede—probably sensing his crumbling will.

"Millie is missing," she said. "Her driver and maid have both been killed."

Edgerton and her mother both went to stone. Then

erupted with dueling shouts: "Why did you not say from the beginning?" and "Where was this?"

Rather than answer their questions, Hugh pressed forward. "We have reason to believe Lady Redding and Lord Cartwright planned to meet here, today. But before that could come to pass, she was abducted, and her servants killed."

A show of genuine emotion gripped the baroness as she squealed and covered her gaping mouth with her hands. "Not my Millie!"

"Cartwright, that good for nothing rapscallion," the baron seethed. "He is behind this!"

"Why would you suggest that?"

"Isn't it obvious?" he blustered. "He is taking out his revenge on us. I thought you were supposed to be the inspector."

Hugh fought a groan. Revenge, after nearly fifteen years? He thought not.

"Uncle, this has nothing to do with you, I'm sure. Millie is the one in danger here, not you," Audrey said. "Can you recall anything she might have said when she was here last? Any indication that she was in trouble?"

The baroness stood, her chin hitching. "Your sister is above reproach. Unlike you, traveling alone with an eligible bachelor, while you are in mourning, no less. Have you no shame?"

"Finding Millie is far more important than heeding mourning rules, Mother."

The woman seethed but held her tongue.

"Find Cartwright and you will find her," the baron said. "Though I doubt she would be associating with the likes of him willingly, now that there's a proposal on the horizon."

Interest streaked down Hugh's spine, and with it, a completely new avenue of possibilities. "She is expecting a proposal of marriage?"

With a haughty arch of her brow, Audrey's mother replied, "Yes. Lord Westbrook has intimated as much."

Audrey regarded him, her expression brightening just as surely as his was. Lord Westbrook had been at Greenbriar when news of the abduction and killing had arrived, and he certainly had not seemed upset about his missing future bride.

"They are attached, Lord Westbrook and Millie?" Audrey asked.

"Not yet." Her mother momentarily seemed to forget her daughter was missing and instead basked in the good news of a potential betrothal. "His wife recently died, and there has been rumor that he has set his hat toward Millie."

"Why would he have said nothing about this at Greenbriar?" Audrey asked, though she was addressing Hugh rather than her mother. The baroness didn't notice or care.

"Because he is a man who knows how to conduct himself properly." Lady Edgerton leveled Hugh with a glare that needed no explaining. In her view, Hugh was not such a man.

"The answer is simple enough," Edgerton said. "Millie and Westbrook were to be engaged, and Cartwright went mad with jealousy."

Hugh could not suppress his groan this time. "Inquiries are not solved by supposition, Lord Edgerton." The people of Hertfordshire were incredibly lucky this man had not been elected as a magistrate. His ego had significantly dulled his powers of logical thinking.

"Am I to believe you and my niece are handling this inquiry? Preposterous!"

It was time to go; the interview was beginning to spiral out of control, becoming muddied by personal grievances and prejudice.

"We will take our leave." Hugh extended his arm toward Audrey. She nodded tightly, as anxious as he was to depart.

"I certainly hope you did not expect an invitation to stay," the baron shouted at their backs with a mean laugh.

Hugh's boots scuffed to a stop at the door's threshold. He would leave the abhorrent man in no doubt of where he stood.

"Lord Edgerton," he said, looking back, "I would sooner visit Dante's ninth circle of hell before resting my arse under your roof."

The baron spluttered and stammered before shouting, "How dare you?"

"How dare *I*?" Hugh slowly turned. As if knowing that he'd started tumbling past the hold on his temper, Audrey said his name, to beckon him back. But it was too late.

"I know what you did, Edgerton. I know where you sent her and why, and if I were a vengeful man, I would contrive a way to see you locked up there. To leave you there to rot for much longer than two years." Stark fury and shock rippled over the baron and baroness's faces. Audrey touched Hugh, closing her fingers gently around his elbow. He exhaled, forcing his temper down to a simmer. "However, small, pathetic men are unworthy of my trouble and my time. As are cold and bitter mothers."

The baroness gasped in offense.

"You utter cur, I should call you out for your insolence!"

"Uncle, no," Audrey said, but Hugh only grinned in amusement.

"Recall my previous dueling opponents, Edgerton, and you may wisely reconsider. I allowed Bartholomew to live. I didn't show the same mercy to Thomas, and I certainly wouldn't for you."

Hugh turned and with Audrey's arm hooked in his, they left through the front door, out onto the drive into a fine misting rain. Audrey pulled him to a stop, her stare a cross between amusement and disbelief. "You didn't need to do that."

"Maybe not, but I sure as hell wanted to."

She pinned her lips, battling a smile. "I don't think you'll be invited back."

"That was the general idea."

Though it was only momentary, her delight brought forth a full smile—the kind that reached her eyes and cut fine lines at the edges. He had never heard her giggle before, but as she did now, a cord tightened in his chest and stomach. If he could inspire her to make that sound more often, he'd do whatever it took. It was the most pleasant thing he'd heard in a long time. Perhaps ever.

The triumph bubbling through him swiftly went flat as the memory of her confession last night cut in, the blade sharp and unforgiving. He held her stare, her smile dissolving as if she knew the turn of his thoughts.

Greer came around the side of the house. She had likely rushed from the servant's entrance as soon as word of the altercation in the drawing room reached the kitchen.

"We are leaving, Your Grace?" Greer's eyes were rounded with awareness, and Hugh imagined the maid was already well apprised of the tension between Audrey and her family.

"Yes, but first..." Audrey paused to look over her shoulder, to where a narrow, rutted lane diverged from the main gravel drive. It disappeared into a stand of trees. "Would you mind if we made a stop on our way to Fournier Downs?"

Traveling all the way to Greenbriar would have taken the rest of the afternoon and evening, and Hugh didn't want to jeopardize the horses in the dark or encounter any highway ruffians. It was safer to wait until daylight.

"A stop where?" he asked.

Audrey gestured toward the rutted lane. "The family graveyard. It's this way."

CHAPTER
EIGHT

Haverfield had never truly felt like home to Audrey. It was where she'd lived most of the year while a child, excepting the rare trip to London when they would occupy the townhome where her father would often stay while Parliament sat. As Audrey grew older, and certainly after she and Philip had married, she had started to look back at her memories with newfound clarity and realized that her parents had not been in love. They had not even really liked each other.

The few memories she'd retained after all these years were of them apart rather than together, and after he'd died, her mother had never truly seemed to mourn the loss of her husband. Perhaps that was because she was already engaging in an affair with her brother-in-law, Peter. The pair of them turned out to be a perfect match, and it left Audrey wondering why and how her father had come to marry her mother in the first place.

What did she truly know of her father?

As Hugh stopped the phaeton next to the brick

columns flanking the entrance to the family plot, she remembered back to when she was younger, and how desperately she had wanted her father and James to still be alive. Her mother and uncle had been at best, neglectful, and at worst, unkind. When she'd been sent away to Shadewell, she'd lamented the loss of Papa and James even more bitterly. Although, she had no true indication that her father would have acted differently than her mother and uncle. Perhaps he still would have sent her away. Maybe James would have grown to be arrogant and stopped doting on her as she grew up.

It was entirely possible her memories of them were romanticized because she had never been given the chance to find out who they would have been. What life could have been like had her father and James not died was a question she had never quit asking; more so when she'd been younger, though less so now.

Greer opted to stay in the hooded phaeton, as the misting rain had not relented. Audrey thought perhaps her maid also suspected she and Hugh might want a few minutes alone.

However, she wasn't certain Hugh would wish to converse with her. Last night, when he had reacted just as poorly as she imagined he would to the truth about Philip, she'd tossed and turned in bed with regret. But she could never have continued to lie to him, no matter how destructive the truth proved to be. He'd been angry, yes, but there had been something more behind his anger. Disappointment, perhaps. And why shouldn't he be disappointed? Audrey felt it too.

"I haven't visited their graves in years," Audrey said softly as they walked a narrow foot path that ran through the graveyard. Trees in full leaf surrounded the two acres that held most of the Edgertons laid to rest over the centuries.

"I don't believe you need to visit a headstone to be able to talk to the person you're missing," Hugh replied, keeping pace beside her.

"Do you talk to your mother?" she asked, intrigued. "Or your father?"

He took a moment to reply. "No. I do think of them though. Lately, I've been trying to remember more about my father. I never thought I would hold his title. His responsibilities. I wish I'd paid more attention to him."

In the spring, Hugh had questioned whether he could be a proper viscount; he'd been concerned he would not be able to rise to the task. She'd known, of course, that he would do well. It was far more difficult being a Bow Street officer, she imagined, than a viscount, but the change in circumstance would still be a trial. He would miss his work fiercely.

The grave markers for her father and James had worn a little; moss had grown along the base of the stones and settled into some of the carved letters. A small vase sat on the ledge of James's grave; it held a recently wilted nosegay. Audrey crouched and touched the browned petals.

"It appears Lady Edgerton does have a heart after all," she said, noting the second date chiseled into the granite. The tenth of August.

"My brother succumbed to his fever first." She shifted her gaze to her father's gravestone. "My father passed the next morning."

Hugh lowered himself into a crouch beside her, his attention on the headstones. He remained quiet as she returned in her mind to that wretchedly hot day. Confined to the upper floors at Haverfield, locked into her nursery with her nanny to keep her safe from the fever James had returned from Eton with, she had drawn pictures to give to her brother when he was well again. He would have just three weeks at home before the term restarted and he'd leave to return to school. During that time, he would take her to the pond and catch frogs, like they always did, and if they had the chance, they would put them in their mother's bedside drawer. She could still remember the frog picture she'd nearly completed when the housekeeper, Mrs. Banks, had finally come to release her from her stuffy prison.

"When I was told that James had died, and that my father had followed him, I didn't understand what that meant. Followed him where? Why would my father leave to follow James when I was still here?" Audrey sighed, noticing that there was no vase of week-old flowers for the late baron's gravestone. Did her mother care so little for him? Or had he done something to anger her?

"So, I left too," she went on, recalling the panicked shouts of her nanny and the maids as her six-year-old legs had sprinted her across the lawns and fields and into the woods, away from the sobbing staff and her insensible mother, still moaning James's name.

"I ran for hours. I was lost but I didn't mind at all, I just had to keep going. I found a deer trail eventually, then a footpath, and then I entered a beautiful field full of wildflowers. A pair of boys was there. One playing with a wooden sword, the other capturing butterflies in a jar. When they saw me, they looked so frightened." Audrey glanced at Hugh, who was watching her, engrossed in her story. "I had burrs in my clothing and in my hair. I had scratches all over my skin from running through the woods. I was a fright, though I didn't know it. But they took me to their mother, and she and her servants doted on me all afternoon, feeding me ices and cake. She wiped away my tears when I told her why I'd run away from home."

The kindness the Duchess of Fournier had shown her that day had changed Audrey; she'd seen what a mother's love should be.

"The boys," Hugh said. "They were Philip and Michael? You had found your way to Fournier Downs?"

Audrey nodded. "They were as brotherly to me as James had been."

Hugh's brow furrowed, and then he straightened his legs and extended his hand to her. She took it, and he helped her stand, her legs uncramping. He kept her hand in his, then drew it to his lips. He kissed the ridge of her knuckles, encased in black lace.

"I am glad you found them," he said. He was in earnest, and for the very first time, her imagination configured a different scenario. One in which she'd entered the flower field and found not Michael and Philip, but a boyish Hugh. He would have been about their same age. What would have happened if she'd met him then?

But all the what ifs could bury her if she let them.

"Philip cannot come back," she whispered. They were completely alone in this graveyard in the wood, but irrationally, she still feared being overheard. Hugh lowered her hand but kept it clasped within his own.

"He is still out there. An axe hanging over our heads," he replied. "If he isn't careful, if he makes one misstep and is discovered…"

Hugh did not need to continue. Countless times, she had thought of the same thing. It was hopeless. Telling Hugh had only cemented what she'd already known.

Audrey pulled her hand from his. She turned away from him, her throat growing thick. "We can go now."

But he recaptured her hand when she tried to step away and pulled her to him. Audrey didn't resist as he wrapped his arms around her and simply held her close, his embrace a shelter she wished to never leave. Leaning into him, she slipped her arms under his, around his torso. His strength, the hard muscle just underneath his coat, both frightened and exhilarated her.

She closed her eyes and let her cheek rest against his chest, uncaring of the mist on his coat. "I know it's silly, but these last few months, whenever I've imagined you holding me like this, it's made me feel better."

His arms tensed, as if to stop her from pulling away. "I've wanted you in my arms like this for much longer than that."

Pleasure warmed her, starting in the very center of her chest and branching out. She'd missed him terribly. And yet, she'd also not wanted to see him. Hadn't wanted to face him and utter the truth that she'd been burying for months. She had allowed him to believe her widowed. That she was grieving. And now, whatever he'd been hoping for in the future, any possibility he'd imagined for them, had been dashed. Yet here he stood, comforting her.

Feeling inordinately selfish, she stiffened and lifted her cheek from his chest. Then stepped from his arms.

"We need to return to Greenbriar," she said quickly, the change of topic awkward. "To question Lord Westbrook."

Hugh inspected her with a level stare. She wondered

what he was thinking; if he would insist that they continue speaking of Philip. Knowing how direct he was, Hugh might even put an end to things here and now. They were in a graveyard, after all. It would be fitting.

He released her arm. "I'll take you and Greer to Fournier House. I'll stay in Low Heath at the Hare and Crown."

She winced. "You won't stay at the manor?"

He breathed in deep and tucked his chin as he exhaled. "You are in mourning, Audrey. I cannot stay under your roof."

"Oh." Naïvely, she had not even thought of that.

A snap of a twig broke the quiet of the family plot. Hugh's eyes narrowed. He tugged her behind him as he simultaneously drew his flintlock and aimed it at the trees bordering the western corner of the graveyard.

"Come out," he commanded. "Slowly."

CHAPTER
NINE

One component of his former life that Hugh had refused to give up was his double flintlock pistol. Gentlemen of the peerage may not have seen a reason to carry a weapon under their fashionable coats, but Hugh's had come in handy too many times to forgo for the sake of "respectability."

What respectability was there in being dead?

He'd spotted the man moving through the trees mere seconds before he'd stepped upon a twig or branch and announced his presence. He wore a long green coat and black hat, allowing him to blend into the vegetation. Had he remained still, Hugh might not have noticed him at all.

With Audrey now positioned safely behind him, he kept the flintlock aimed as the man emerged, both of his hands raised into the air in capitulation.

"I am unarmed," he called. A few steps into the family plot, and Hugh knew who he must be. His brown skin and gentleman's clothing pointed to one possibility.

"Cartwright."

Lord Montague's grandson started to lower his hands, but Hugh jerked the pistol. "Keep them raised." Cartwright obeyed. "Open your coat."

"I told you, I am unarmed," he replied, though doing as instructed. Seeing no weapon, Hugh lowered his and slipped it back into its holster.

"Lord Cartwright, where is my sister?" Audrey asked, moving out from behind Hugh's shoulder. He tried to nudge her back into place, but she only huffed in annoyance. "Lady Redding," she clarified.

Cartwright, who looked to be in his mid-thirties, stepped forward eagerly. "She is supposed to be here. I have been waiting since dawn. I heard voices and..." He peered at Audrey. "You are Millie's sister. The duchess?"

"Did Lady Redding agree to meet you here?" Hugh asked, wanting to stay on point. He didn't entirely trust that Cartwright was in earnest. Skulking about in the woods made him look damned suspicious.

"And may I ask who you are, sir?" he asked Hugh, appearing just as suspicious of him.

Hugh tensed. He abhorred introducing himself these days. "Viscount Neatham."

Cartwright considered this with an arch of one brow, and then answered Hugh's question. "We were going to meet here, yes. Then announce our engagement to the baron and Lady Edgerton." He shifted his footing and peered toward the graveyard gate, almost warily. "Where is Millie?"

"We don't know," Audrey answered. "She is missing."

Cartwright surged forward, his alarm seemingly genuine. "Missing? What happened? How do you know this?"

"Her carriage was set upon yesterday, her driver killed," Hugh explained. "Then, shortly after, her maid's body was pulled from a river not far from where Lady Redding was abducted."

Cartwright swiped his hat from his head, revealing a crop of waved raven hair. "Abducted? Saints alive... We must go. We must find her."

With his eyes wide with panic, Hugh began to doubt that the man was acting. But he also wasn't telling them everything.

"The last letter you received from Lady Redding...what did it say?"

"What does that matter?" Cartwright's temper climbed alongside his worry. "If Millie is missing, I must find her. Where was her carriage when it was attacked?"

"Kent. Near an estate called Greenbriar," Audrey answered. "But we must know what her last letter said to you. That she would come here? That she would marry you? Even after the baron and our mother refused the match?"

"To hell with the baron and baroness!" His voice ricocheted through the family plot, startling a clutch of birds in the tree limbs. Sudden quiet followed their trilling and flapping wings. Cartwright closed his eyes, visibly calming with a long exhalation. "I'm sorry. I cannot conceal my rancor for them."

"We've just learned of their rejection of your proposal for my sister fifteen years ago," Audrey said, sympathy gentling her voice. "We also found your letters to Millie at Reddingate. Our intent wasn't to trespass, but to find out why she would have set out for Greenbriar rather than Haverfield, as she told her staff."

He gripped the brim of his hat and shook his head. "I don't know. My last letter to her was a request to meet me here, today. She replied saying she would. That she did not care what her mother or uncle said this time. She no longer had to bend to their will."

"The Viscount Redding has been dead for four years," Hugh said, not satisfied by Cartwright's answers so far. "Why wait for so long to propose to her again?"

Cartwright hardened, his dark brown eyes filling with contempt. "I have been in India for well over a decade. There was nothing here in England for me, not after I lost Millie. By the time I learned of the viscount's death, it had already been three years. For a short while, I worried she had remarried. Presumed she had. But then, I wrote to her, on the off chance, and...she said she had not."

Hugh relaxed somewhat. Cartwright was in love with Lady Redding, there was no doubt of that. The subtle shifts of his expression when he spoke of her revealed it; an affection he couldn't conceal. However, all they had were his letters to Millie, and only his word on what her replies had been. If she had not felt the same way, or if she had not agreed to meet him here to announce their engagement, that might explain why she had been traveling in the opposite direction. To get away from him.

"She still cared for you?" Audrey asked, encouraging him to continue.

"She did. Millie believed I must have married, moved on. But I've only ever loved her."

Wonderment filled Audrey's eyes and parted her lips as she simply stared at Cartwright. Hugh had never made the viscountess's acquaintance, but he found he held preconceived notions about her; they weren't too far from his notions about the baron and Lady Edgerton. But perhaps Cartwright knew Millie in ways Audrey did not.

"Your grandfather is Lord Montague," Hugh said as he saw more movement from the corner of his eye. It was only Greer, coming into the family plot, likely having heard Cartwright's shouting. Audrey signaled to her that all was well.

"I have the misfortune of calling him grandfather, yes," he scowled. "The man despises me as deeply as I despise him. I haven't seen or spoken to him in as long as I've been overseas."

"How would he feel about your betrothal to Lady Redding now?"

Cartwright scoffed. "I don't care what he would feel. I have made my fortune, free of my grandfather's estates, on my own terms. I have no need for him or his approval."

"Is there anyone who would object to your marriage?" Hugh asked. "Any other family members?"

The man sighed heavily, his impatience brimming. Hugh could understand; if someone were to tell him Audrey was missing, he would not want to stand around answering questions.

"My cousin, Mr. Robert Henley. I do not think he would care one way or another, but he is the only other family I have. His father, my uncle, died years ago. I'm sure grandfather would much rather Henley be his heir, rather than me. He at least looks the part."

White, Hugh assumed him to mean. Hugh did not know of Mr. Henley but would ask Thornton tomorrow as soon as they arrived at Greenbriar.

"In one of your last letters," Audrey said, and by her pinched look of concentration, Hugh could tell she was piecing something together in her mind. "You asked Millie if she still had something. What was it?"

When Cartwright hesitated to answer, she cocked her head, her black bonnet dusted silver with the misty rainfall. "A ring perhaps?" she prodded.

The abductors had demanded the ring, according to Audrey's vision. With all that they'd learned about a past rejected proposal and a new one on the horizon—from both Cartwright and Lord Westbrook—the mention of a ring didn't seem so out of the ordinary now.

Cartwright, as garrulous as he'd been so far, was now reticent.

"To find Lady Redding, we need all the information you have," Hugh reminded him.

Cartwright changed his hat from one hand to the other, then placed it on his head, his hair now damp. "Yes. A ring. *My* ring, though my grandfather would disagree with that."

"How so?"

"My father gave my mother a rare purple diamond when they married in Kochi, India. When they died of fever and I was sent to England, their possessions came with me. The diamond was among them. Grandfather placed the ring in his safe, and when I planned to propose to Millie, I asked for it. It was my mother's. I know she would have wanted me to give it to the woman I wished to marry. But he refused, saying that the ring belonged to him."

Hugh crossed his arms. "Let me guess—you took it anyway."

The sly crook of Cartwright's head was his answer. "And my loving grandfather had me arrested for thievery."

Now this was getting interesting.

"The charges were dropped, of course, when my solicitor convinced the magistrates that I was the rightful owner of the diamond, but Grandfather was not satisfied."

The pattering of rain on the leaves of the trees surrounding the family plot increased. The three of them would become soaked if they stayed out here much longer.

"Where is the ring now?" Audrey asked, seemingly oblivious to the weather.

"Millie tried to give it back to me, but I wanted her to keep it."

"Even after she rejected your proposal?"

"I could never have offered my mother's diamond to anyone else. I told her that the ring was hers, just as my heart was hers. One day, she would be my wife. No matter how long it took."

The man's devotion bordered on delusion. But then, how many times had Hugh himself considered that no woman he met could ever hold a candle to Audrey? Perhaps it wasn't so delusional at all.

And with a cold clap of certainty, he knew that he would never want another. So, what was he to do? Walk away from Audrey out of fear that Philip would return? Looking at Cartwright now, a man past his prime, his hair graying, Hugh felt pity. The man had spent the last fifteen years lamenting the loss of the woman he loved. He didn't want that for himself.

"So, Millie still has the ring," Audrey surmised, pulling Hugh from his dismal thoughts. "Who else is aware of this?"

"Just me. I suppose my valet back then probably knew. Valets know everything, of course. My grandfather likely believed I've had possession of it all these years." Cartwright paced a tight circle, his agitation and impatience boiling over. "I cannot stay. I will ride for Kent and Greenbriar."

"We are leaving at dawn," Hugh said. "It will be nightfall long before you reach Kent. Traveling the roads wouldn't be wise. Meet us tomorrow at sunrise at the Hare and Crown in Low Heath."

He could see what Cartwright thought of that by the glare he spared him.

"Where is your old valet now?" Hugh asked.

"I couldn't begin to say. I haven't heard from him since I quit my grandfather's home." Then, he turned on his heel and broke for the woods again. "I am staying at the Hare and Crown as well. Tomorrow, not one minute past dawn. Otherwise, I ride for Kent alone."

Then, with a belated tip of his hat toward Audrey, he hurried back into the trees.

"Someone else knows he gave Millie that diamond," she said as he went, "if the abductors were looking for it."

"It could have been Montague's men." Hugh thought it the most likely answer. Then again, the most likely answer wasn't always the correct one. It was simply the easiest.

"Or the valet recently said something to the wrong person," Audrey suggested as they turned back toward the gates. Greer still stood there, waiting for her mistress. "Or else why would someone wait until right now to track down Millie for it? She's had it for fifteen years already."

"*If* she still has it," Hugh said. "It would be worth a fortune. And if she never thought she'd see Cartwright again, she could have sold it. What if she panicked when he asked her to bring it?"

It was a true muddle, and by the bleak and bewildered way Audrey rubbed at her temple, she had as few answers as Hugh did. Just endless questions and a troubling fear that Lady Redding may already be beyond help.

CHAPTER

TEN

G reer had left Audrey's bedchamber for her usual room in the servant's wing at Fournier House hours ago. Though she tried to fall asleep, Audrey's mind was too alert, her limbs restless. She felt much like how Lord Cartwright must—impatient to move. The longer they took to track Millie down, the worse the chances that she would come to no harm.

But Hugh had been right to insist they stay put for the night. Traveling pitch black country roads would not only be potentially dangerous for them, but also for the horses. Still, no amount of logic could diminish her worry.

Hers was likely the only lamp in the house still lit when the clock's hands started past the two o'clock hour. Reading usually made her eyes tired enough to tempt her into sleep, but it wasn't working this time. She couldn't concentrate on the words, and in fact, several times she even forgot the title of the book. Finally, she snapped it shut and tossed it across the bed, toward her feet.

Greer had left the window sash open at Audrey's request.

Though the staff had been prepared for their arrival, as she should have arrived the day before, her room had been stuffy after being battened up for most of the summer. Genie had thoughtfully sent a messenger to Mrs. Anders, the house-keeper at Fournier House, to alert the staff that their mistress would be delayed for an indeterminate length of time. She'd included no mention of the predicament, and for that, Audrey was grateful. She would address the staff in the morning, to explain the reason for her hasty departure back to Greenbriar.

A breeze, scented with fresh rain and clipped grass, came through the open window. As did a rhythmic noise. Audrey held still, listening as it grew louder. The source was unmistakable: a horse and rig were coming fast up the drive.

She tossed off the thin counterpane and went to peer out the window. The butler at Fournier House, Verly, always instructed the footmen to leave a few lamps burning at the front entrance to the house, and the light soon illuminated a familiar horse, phaeton, and driver.

Audrey dashed to her banyan, draped on the foot of her bed, and threw it on as she left her room. Hugh had left for Low Heath just after supper; to come racing back at this time of night could only mean one thing: grave news.

As she rushed to the foyer, her mind went oddly blank, unable to even deliberate what the news might be. The footmen and Verly had turned in for the night, but Hugh's arrival had not gone unnoticed. Scuffing footfalls from deeper within the house reached her ears as Audrey opened the front door.

She stepped onto the paving stones just beyond the door, the night air damp and scented with rose and gardenia. The flames in the sconces trembled as Hugh jumped from the phaeton and cut a swift line toward her.

"Is everything well here?" he asked, short on breath, his attention shifting to the outside exterior of the house, then over her shoulder where Verly now approached.

"Here? Yes, everything is fine. But what has happened?" Audrey stepped aside and allowed him in.

"I will have your horse and phaeton seen to, my lord," Verly said to Hugh before closing the door and locking it. He set his lantern on the credenza to give them light, and then left on his task to wake a footman.

Hugh wore no hat for the butler to take, and on second inspection, Audrey realized he also wore no waistcoat or cravat. In his coat, trousers, and white muslin shirt, he looked as if he'd been shaken awake in his bed by some midnight emergency.

He looked around the large foyer, as if expecting to find someone. "Was Cartwright here?"

"Of course not. I thought he was staying at the Crown and Hare, like you."

Tension fled Hugh's shoulders, and he reached to rub the back of his neck. "He was. I saw him when I arrived at the posting inn. He was on his way to his room. I slept for a short while, then awoke. There was some noise, a muffled argument. I couldn't get back to sleep, and I had questions for Cartwright, so I went to see if he was still awake. I found his door already open. He was gone."

"Gone?"

"The place was a wreck. It had been turned over."

Too stunned to speak, Audrey's mind raced as she took the lantern Verly had left and led Hugh to the drawing room.

There, their voices might not be overheard by the few waking servants. Verly and Mrs. Anders had reduced the staff by half, considering Audrey could host no guests or social events for the rest of the summer.

She brightened the lantern after setting it down, and then turned to Hugh. "Someone was searching for the diamond? And they've now abducted Lord Cartwright?"

Skepticism was so familiar an expression for him, it had carved its own pleat in his left cheek. "Or Cartwright turned the place over himself. Made it look like an abduction."

Audrey didn't believe it. "Why would he do such a thing?"

She had not been in Lord Cartwright's presence for more than fifteen minutes that afternoon, but to fake his own abduction made little sense, especially when his primary goal was to find Millie.

Though, perhaps he also wanted to find the ring. Causing a scene such as the one at the Hare and Crown could have been done with the intent to confuse and slow Audrey and Hugh or redirect them.

Hugh shook his head. "The diamond is important to someone. In your vision, Millie said she didn't have it?"

That vision had cycled through Audrey's mind again and again as she'd mined it for anything she'd missed. But there was no question. "Millie wasn't lying. She was terrified. In that state, she would have handed it over if she'd had it."

Hugh paced, raking his hand through his already tousled hair, and mussing it even further. His rumpled appearance sent a bolt of warmth through her. And then, of heartache.

"I'm glad you're safe," he said, unaware of her reaction to

him. "I thought perhaps Cartwright or whoever went through his room might think to come here next to search."

She would have considered that too; it would behoove Millie's abductors to take into account her family and any place she might have stored the ring. However, it was no great secret to anyone who paid attention that Audrey and Millie were not close. Audrey would be the last person Millie would entrust with such a gemstone.

If, as Hugh had questioned earlier, she even still possessed it.

"I will have a room prepared for you," Audrey said. She was ready to stand her ground and refuse to let him return to Low Heath for the few remaining hours before sunrise.

But he didn't argue. Not that point anyhow.

"I'll stay in here if you don't object. I'd like to be on the ground floor. Just in case."

"I do have footmen who can guard the door."

"Your footmen don't have pistols," Hugh replied, patting his coat at the hip. "Besides, I likely won't sleep from here on out."

Mrs. Anders appeared in the drawing room entrance in her sleeping cap and robe, asking if they'd like tea prepared, but Audrey declined and sent her back to bed. Alone again, she crossed to the table holding a tray of decanters and poured them both a finger of whisky.

"I likely won't sleep now either," she said, handing Hugh his glass.

He removed his coat and laid it over the arm of the sofa before sitting down. Audrey settled herself at the opposite end. Mrs. Anders had apparently already awoken a maid, Maggie, who now appeared and set about building a fire in the hearth. They sipped their whiskies in silence as the young woman, probably still half-asleep, worked. Audrey caught Hugh's glances a few times across the stretch of silk cushion between them, his attention once drifting toward her bare feet. She had rushed downstairs in such a hurry, she'd forgone her slippers. Audrey raised her legs and tucked them underneath her, to which his lips curled into a sly grin before taking another sip.

"Thank you, Maggie," Audrey said as the maid finished. She bobbed a curtsey and then left, likely eager to return to her bed.

"You know all your servants by name." It was an observation, not a question.

"I've always tried to. The staff has been reduced this summer, of course. That makes the task simpler." She smiled and swirled the whisky in her glass, the previous sip having left a pleasant heat in her chest.

"Basil is after me to hire a full staff and leave Bedford Street for Kensington Square."

"Neatham House is yours now. And entailed, I presume?" Hugh nodded though he didn't look especially pleased. He'd had plenty of time to take up residence, yet he hadn't. "You don't wish to live there?"

He leaned back into the corner of the sofa, visibly relaxing. "The place doesn't hold the fondest memories. I never felt as though I belonged there. No, I would rather lease it and stay on Bedford Street for now."

She could understand. "I've never felt as if I belonged here, either. Or even at Violet House."

The lift of his chin showed his interest in the statement,

and she wished she'd held her tongue. She'd never told anyone that. Not even Philip.

"Why?"

The contents of her whisky glass were low, her limbs loosening. The flames in the hearth cast the room in change-able firelight as she considered her answer.

"I think it is because our marriage was a sham." She kept her voice soft on the off-chance Verly had placed a footman in the foyer, to be easily summoned. "And I felt like a sham of a duchess."

The corner of Hugh's mouth twitched, but his expression remained flat. He knew the truth of their marriage. That it had never been consummated, and why. That should not have kept Audrey from feeling like the lady of the house—she'd told herself that countless times. And yet, it had. It still did.

"I feel as if I tricked my way into this position, and I can't help but now feel like a burden to the staff."

Instead of telling her that she was wrong to feel as she did, he said, "You plan to move out, then?"

"There is a dower house here, and in London, Michael and Genie will certainly want to move into Violet House before winter..." She left off and shrugged a shoulder. "I suppose I don't have many options left to me."

She felt suspended in time. Waiting.

A knob formed in her throat, and quickly, Audrey drank the rest of her whisky.

"He is with someone?" Hugh asked after a few moments of quiet. She knew who he referred to.

Her throat was too cinched to speak Mr. Frederick Walk-er's name, but she confirmed with a nod.

"What happens when he decides it is over? When he deems it time to come back?" Hugh was only voicing what Audrey herself had pondered when Philip first told her his plan. But since then, her fear had subsided. For logical reasons, too.

"He won't," she replied softly. "He *can't*. He would face charges of fraud for falsifying his death, he'd destroy the Fournier name. It would be beyond cruel of him to turn up again after letting his brothers and sister believe he is dead. He isn't cruel—"

"How can you defend him?" Hugh cut in. "He was cruel to put this on your shoulders, to leave you to play the part of widow and to uphold his lie. If you dare speak the truth, *you* choose to injure Michael and Cassie and Tobias, *you* choose to destroy the family name. You are the one who will be ruined, not Philip. Yet, he didn't care, did he?"

Even as his scathing words battered her, they were familiar. He was saying nothing that she had not already thought to herself in the many moments of deep frustration since Philip's departure.

And yet, she still loved him, his flaws and all. They were both responsible for their decision to marry. At the time, it had been a genius idea. Audrey would not have to marry Lord Bainbury, twice her age and arranged by her detestable uncle. And Philip would have a wife who knew his truth and would never ask for what he could not give. The possibility of taking lovers had been agreed upon. But their arrangement had been imperfect; they had not taken into account what they would do if they each one day fell in love, rather than just lust.

"You don't know him as I do. He does care," Audrey

said. "He made me a vow. He will never return and put my new life in jeopardy, and I trust him. I know you do not, but *I do*. I also know he believed he was doing the only thing he could to give us each a chance at happiness."

Then again, Hugh's predilection for blunt honesty had forced her to acknowledge there were two sides to Philip's actions. He had wanted to give her the chance to marry for love. But Philip had not understood that the man she wanted would not have her once he knew she was not truly widowed. Philip had not understood that Audrey couldn't simply lie to Hugh and let him be blissfully unaware. She could never betray him that way. Tears of frustration stung her eyes.

"Bollocks," Hugh scoffed. "He was not thinking of your happiness. He was thinking of his own. Hell, if you're not going to be angry on your own behalf, then I will be."

"I am angry!" Her cry pierced the air, which until that moment had been filled with nothing but cautious, harsh whispers. She stood from the sofa and clenched her hands into fists but felt utterly powerless. "I'm furious, but not just with Philip. With myself and my choices, and with this whole bloody world and the rules we must abide by, and the terrible luck of falling in love with you when it would have been so much simpler to feel nothing at all!"

She sucked in a sharp breath the very moment those last words had flown from her tongue. Hugh's livid scowl went slack as Audrey backed up a step. She'd said too much.

"Audrey—"

"No, I shouldn't have...I need to...forgive me, goodnight."

The awkwardness of her abrupt departure didn't fully strike her until she was on the steps to the first floor. She barely took a breath as she rushed headlong toward her room. What a fool she'd been! The confession of love had appeared from nowhere, slinking out from the corner of her mind where it had been kept tucked away, safe and secret. What good could come of saying it now?

Stinging tears fell freely as she shut her bedchamber door and leaned against it. She swiped them away. So rarely did she give in to emotion that her wet cheeks infuriated her. Crying would achieve nothing. So why could she not stem them?

Philip's promise to never return, to allow her to move on with her life without fear of his deception being made known, would never be enough, not for Hugh. He had seen the destruction of a bigamous marriage firsthand with his own father and stepmother. He would never risk such a thing himself.

"Audrey."

Hugh's voice came through the wood at her back. He'd followed her. A jolt of pleasure, and one of dread, chimed through her. He hadn't knocked, likely knowing the sound might carry. "Don't run away from me. Please, open the door."

It wasn't locked. He could turn the knob himself, but instead he waited for her to choose to let him in or not. She composed herself, angrily wiping the tears that had wet her cheeks. Evidence of them would still linger, but she couldn't leave a man in the upstairs landing for a servant to come upon. She opened the door, and immediately, Hugh crossed the threshold, forcing her back a few steps. He took the door from her hand, shut it behind him, and without stopping to so much as speak, his arms came around her. Hugh bent to capture her lips, stealing her breath with the insistent press of his mouth. Initial shock melted beneath his kiss, and Audrey gripped his shoulders to keep her legs steady.

"Why did you do that?" she asked when their lips parted, though he remained close enough for the tips of their noses to touch. "You're supposed to be angry with me."

"I am," he said, then pulled back to see her better. She noted the lack of ire in his eyes now, the wrath he'd displayed in the drawing room seemingly exhausted. He drew his thumb over the curve of her lower lip. "I am also in love with you."

The words tolled through her and drove out her next breath.

"But I thought you wouldn't accept... Your principles, they're..." Her breath wasn't the only thing to have scattered, apparently. Coherent words were lost as well.

"Principle. Yes, there is that. And I've clung to it." He tucked a strand of hair framing her face behind her ear. "Perhaps too tightly. But what you said is true. He cannot come back. Not now. I don't believe him to be a fool, and regardless of what I said in anger downstairs, I don't believe he is cruel. Selfish in many ways, yes," he said, still holding her, keeping her from floating toward the ceiling, for she'd started to feel light as air. "But not too long ago, he was willing to go to the gallows to preserve his secret. The damage *this* secret would cause would be even more severe. He won't risk it."

Everything Hugh was saying was a revelation, but as Audrey stared at his mouth, she only wanted it to form those few precious words again: *I'm in love with you.* She wanted to be certain she hadn't imagined them. But instead, his lips lowered to press against hers. Audrey draped her arms around his shoulders and reveled in the tender kiss.

"Come what may, whatever the risk, I have made my choice: I am not giving you up. I cannot," he said, his lips moving against hers as he spoke. Decadent, weightless sensations filled her. Relief. Joy. Exhilaration. She had expected none of these.

"But...what happened with your father and mother and stepmother—"

"That was different." He shook his head, his nose brushing against hers. "April Barlow deceived them both, and she felt no remorse. Just as Esther Starborough and Doctor Warwick deceived Mr. Starborough." The horrible murder and blackmail situation from last November had involved a selfish couple who'd led a man to believe his wife was dead, so that they may start a new life and family together. Their tragic situation had crossed her mind many times the last few months.

Hugh continued. "Philip was honest with you, and you are being honest with me. There are no lies between us. Between the three of us, I should say."

"But I am still helping him to deceive other people. Michael and Genie, Cassandra and Tobias...the House of Lords, for heaven's sake."

"Do you plan to marry any of them?"

Audrey widened her eyes, and her heart tripped to a stop. She all but croaked, "Marry?"

With a wicked grin, Hugh touched his nose to hers again. This close, his presence was overpowering. "It is what I want."

As close as his confession took her to it, she refused to swoon. Not until she laid out one last crucial truth. "But we will both know that I am still married. That we are not truly wed."

"Did Philip ever make you his wife in truth?"

He held her stare, waiting, even though he already knew the answer. Slowly, she shook her head.

"Audrey," he began, his dark brown eyes simmering to a deep umber. "I intend to make you my wife. My wife, in full," he added, with a roguish arch of his brow. She thought it entirely possible she might expire, there and then, from a profusion of pleasure. Of undiluted bliss igniting in the very center of her soul.

Following base desire, Audrey nudged her lips closer, kissing him. She stood on the tips of her toes, and Hugh's arms, already encircling her, flexed. He held her so securely that although she tried to drop her heels back to the carpet, they did not. Her toes remained hovering over the floor. The muscles underneath his shirt could have been steel plated for how firm they felt against her. He held her as if she were a treasure that he feared would be stolen away. In his arms like this, she felt safeguarded against any possible evil.

Her temperature rose, and her pulse knocked in her neck. He kept her sealed to his chest and abdomen with one powerful arm, while the other lowered to the sash tying her banyan. She pulled her lips from his with a small intake of air.

"I don't want you to regret anything. I don't want you to regret me," she said, laying bare her deepest fear.

Hugh cocked his head. "The only thing I could possibly regret would be not giving us a chance."

Audrey swallowed a sob of relief. She had fully expected him to walk away, to tell her he would not compromise. He kissed her then, the heat of it chasing away the sob. And when he tugged the sash of her robe, loosening it to allow the banyan's panels to open, she forgot to breathe.

"Your mourning period doesn't end for another nine months," he said, his hand touching down on her hip, his palm warming her skin through the muslin nightgown. "If you would prefer to wait until then for me to stay—"

"No." The word rushed out, barely formed, barely perceptible. Clawing for what remained of her senses and dignity, she swallowed and said more clearly, "No, I don't prefer that."

Hugh's answering grin revealed he'd been hoping for that response, and that he knew exactly what she was feeling inside. Her longing for him, to love him in the way she never thought she'd love anyone. To let him love her, touch her, in the way she feared he never would.

The satin banyan slipped from her shoulders and fell to the carpet at her feet under the gentlest tug of his hands. Then, in a rush of motion, Hugh bent and swept her legs out from under her while bracing her back. Locked in his arms, Audrey hooked her hands around his nape. She'd often wondered what it might feel like to run her fingers through those dark, glossy strands, and so she learned that his hair was thick and soft as he carried her to her bed, his gaze steady on hers. The gravity of his stare was slightly alarming. He had looked at her with longing before, but this was something altogether different. This look *seared*. He was going to make love to her, and while she would rather the world end than stop him and send him from her room now, the barest doubt lingered.

He must have recognized it in her eyes, or in the way her arms went rigid around his neck. Hugh stopped as he reached the bedside, and still cradling her, said, "You are nervous."

"A little." There was no point denying it.

"You trust me?"

"Yes," she said without hesitation. Then, with a coy grin, "You have saved my life a few times, after all."

The corner of his mouth rose, dimpling his cheek. He kissed her languidly while lowering her feet to the floor. Her skin prickled everywhere as he bunched the muslin at her thighs and in unhurried torment, began to lift the gown's hem.

"We'll go slowly," he said in the half-second his lips were parted from hers. "Tell me to stop, and I will."

But she already knew she wouldn't want that. Her trepidation wasn't rooted in fear of the actual act; it was in how things between them might change afterward. Up until this point, she had known one part of Hugh. Now, she would know another. She didn't want that to change them. Unless it was for the better.

Audrey lifted her arms, and with her heart in her throat, he drew the gown over her head and off her fingertips. Cool air from the open window kissed the backs of her thighs and the bare skin between her shoulders as the cloud of muslin cleared her vision. Once again, she was looking into Hugh's eyes. His heated gaze lowered, though only briefly, respectful as he was of her nervousness.

His hands brushed down her arms, raising gooseflesh, and then curled over her hips. "You are as gorgeous as I imagined you would be."

Audrey bit her lower lip to stop her preening grin. "And you are still clothed, Mr. Marsden."

He kissed her throat, then her shoulder, as his hands traveled the bare expanse of her backside, sending shivers of delight and need through her. "Don't you mean, *my lord*?" he whispered against her earlobe.

The bit of humor put her at ease, and Audrey reached for his shirt. As she tugged it from the waist of his trousers and her palms flattened against the warm, smooth skin of his abdomen, her hesitation all but vanished. There was nothing for her to worry over. Hugh was already her partner in so many ways. This would simply be one more.

When they were equally undressed, and Audrey had admired Hugh's impressive form through bashful glances, he lowered her to the bed. In that moment, nothing she'd experienced in the whole of her life had ever felt so right or so beautiful. As promised, he moved slowly, telling her between kisses what would come next. Restraint deepened his voice and tensed his muscles as he held himself in control. When the dashing pain faded, however, she whispered to him to let go. And at last, they came together in a rapture of long hindered desire, every touch one of reverence, every gasping breath a promise of devotion. He sighed her name with a vulnerability she'd never dreamed he'd show her, and when the world collapsed around them in shattering sparks of light, his kisses swallowed her nonsensical whimpers.

Later, as the sun rose and gilded the counterpane covering them, they lay sated and sleepy in each other's arms. It was then, while resting her head against Hugh's chest and listening to his heartbeat that Audrey finally understood true happiness. She'd found it. This was her chance. And come what may, she would not let go.

ELEVEN

Hugh directed the horses onto the long, winding lane that led to Greenbriar just as the bloated white clouds that had been drifting across the sky all afternoon turned an ominous gray. The winds increased, whipping leaves over to show their silvery backsides. They had been traveling the heavier trafficked post road and sparser country lanes since earlier that morning, only stopping once to change out the horses and eat, though both tasks had been hurried. They were too eager to reach Greenbriar and learn what more had been discovered since they left to engage in much conversation along the way. And considering Greer sat between them, nothing could be said about the exquisite early morning hours he and Audrey had spent together.

Traveling with Greer had been slightly awkward at first, especially since the maid had quietly entered the bedchamber just past dawn to wake her mistress and prepare for their early departure. Hugh had already been awake, reclining on pillows with a sleeping Audrey curled up against his side, her rhythmic breaths gusting across his bare chest. Greer, ever tactful, had immediately retreated and snicked the door shut behind her. He'd decided not to mention it to Audrey when she woke; she would have only been mortified. And upon her waking, he'd been too distracted by her to think of her maid anyhow.

Hell, he could still feel her bare legs shifting over his as she stirred and stretched, her cheek turning against his chest as she craned her neck to look up at him. With her hair in loosed waves of golden silk, her lips still pink and swollen from his mouth, she'd been irresistible. Making love to her again in the full morning sunlight, hearing those soft sounds she made that drove him to the brink of madness, he'd decided then and there that they would never leave her bed. The rest of the world could burn, and he wouldn't give a damn.

"I didn't know this feeling was even possible," she'd whispered after as she lay loose-limbed in his arms, dropping kisses along his chest and skimming her foot up his shin.

"Neither did I," he'd replied, to which her foot suddenly went still. She'd lifted herself up and rested her chin on his pectoral.

"I am not naïve, Hugh. I know you've been with other women."

She hadn't asked for details. Had she done so, he would have been honest and told her about Gloria Hanson, the mistress he'd kept for nearly two years. They had been companions, nothing more. No deep feelings had been involved, other than pleasure. That was what made everything with Audrey different. And to his expanding wonder, infinitely more fulfilling.

"Yes. However, never with a woman I am in love with,"

he'd said to her in earnest. "This is a different feeling entire-ly." And it was. He felt exultant, yet also like he was standing on the edge of a cliff. There could be no turning back now, and nor did he wish to.

She'd valiantly fought a pleased grin.

"You truly haven't been in love?"

He hadn't needed to mull over the question for long. When he recalled the women that he'd taken an interest in before, and what he felt for Audrey, there was no comparison.

"Not until you."

The eager way she'd rewarded him for that confession had kept his blood boiling for nearly the whole ride to Kent.

On second thought, it was a saving grace Greer was with them in the phaeton. Had she not been, Hugh certainly would have given in to the temptation of pulling over and dragging Audrey into a roadside thicket.

But now, as they closed in on Greenbriar and the house party that would be underway, he set all wicked thoughts of her aside and concentrated on the conflict at hand. With any hope, Lady Redding would have turned up during the two days they had been gone. But a gut feeling said it wasn't to be so.

A greeting party awaited them as they approached the front entrance, a footman likely having spied the phaeton crossing the arched stone bridge over the brook, which had a clear prospect of the home. The new duchess, Genie, and Lady Cassandra were joined by Thornton and a handful of footmen. The servants took the traces and saw to the horses and phaeton after Hugh had helped Audrey and Greer down.

"Any news of Millie?" Audrey asked as soon as Genie released her from an embrace.

The downward turn of Genie's mouth preceded the shake of her head. "I am afraid not." She grasped Audrey's hands. "I take it she was not at Reddingate."

"Nor at Haverfield or Fournier Downs," Hugh provided as he caught a shrewd look from Thornton. Sir had certainly spoke to him, telling him of Cartwright and asking what he knew of the man. It appeared he had something to convey.

Lady Cassandra and Genie each took one of Audrey's arms, bracketing her, and they began toward the front entrance. Hugh and Thornton followed them slowly.

"Sir said Lord Cartwright has something to do with this. "

"Yes. I take it Cartwright doesn't precede us?" When Thornton frowned, Hugh released his faint hope of finding the man here.

"No. Why?"

"Between us," Hugh prefaced, "Cartwright had written letters of endearment to Lady Redding. Several. The last was a request to meet at Haverfield yesterday to announce their intent to marry. Edgerton and Audrey's mother were ignorant to the whole affair, and of course the viscountess never arrived. Cartwright, however, was there. Audrey and I spoke to him."

Hugh briefly explained about Lord Montague having Cartwright arrested for taking the rare diamond ring with which he'd proposed to Millie the first time, of Cartwright letting her keep it, and then of how she was to bring it with her to Haverfield.

"Someone knew she had it on her?" Thornton deduced

as they neared the entrance, the door held open by a foot-man. "That is why her carriage was set upon?"

Hugh clenched his back teeth. He'd anticipated that he'd need to find a way around telling his friend of Audrey's vision, and now hoped what he'd settled on was enough.

"If she had it with her, I fear she would have been found dead alongside her driver. Instead, she was abducted. I believe it is because she didn't have it."

"But knew where it was," Thornton said, catching on without any reservations about Hugh's theory. "Perhaps her maid was killed as a punishment, because Lady Redding refused to give up the location of the diamond?"

The suggestion was reasonable, and if Hugh didn't know better, he would have considered it. But what Audrey had seen while holding the maid's cross pendant effectively wiped out that theory. Celine Woods had betrayed Millie somehow, and it likely had to do with either the ring, or the secret letters from Cartwright. Not that he could say any of this to his friend. However, he did explain how Cartwright was now missing too, and the state of his room.

Doubt crept over Thornton's face. "Could he have done it himself? Maybe he only wants the diamond back and is involved in Lady Redding's disappearance somehow."

Hugh had considered the same. "But why stage such a scene? Why not just leave in the middle of the night to return to wherever he was keeping the viscountess?"

Thornton shrugged. "All I know of the man is what you've said: he was arrested for stealing from his own grand-father. Shortly after, he left with the East India Company."

"From what Cartwright said, Lord Montague is a peevish

old man who despised his heir's decision to wed an Indian woman and produce a mixed-race son," Hugh said.

"Montague is known as a recluse. Rumor is that after his only two children died, he tucked himself away from society."

The first drops of rain struck Hugh's nose and forehead, and he and Thornton made their way into the house just before the clouds unleashed a torrent. In the large, open foyer, the ladies were meeting with several more guests, including Fournier and Lords Kettleridge and Westbrook. As Basil stepped forward to take Hugh's coat, hat, and driving gloves to be cleaned of road dust, he saw Audrey inspecting Westbrook, her lips pinched, and eyes narrowed.

"The magistrate, Sir Ridley Harrow, has taken possession of the driver's body and that of the maid's," Fournier said with no pre-amble. Something Hugh appreciated. "He's arranged a double inquest in Moorsly tomorrow to determine cause of death, though it's sure to be only ceremonial. There is no doubt both are murder."

The duke's expression was drawn with concern, and he looked to have suffered a few sleepless nights.

"We've launched a search of the parkland and surrounding villages," Kettleridge said, his interest bright at the unexpected commotion and mystery. Unlike Westbrook, whose sour expression hinted that he saw the upheaval at Greenbriar as a nuisance. Lady Edgerton's prideful remarks about the man planning to propose to her daughter appeared baseless on the surface.

"Several farmers have volunteered as well," Fournier added. "They've been combing the woods and fields." With an apologetic glance at Audrey, he added, "To no avail."

At least they had not yet found a body. Considering the driver and maid were so easily found, it gave Hugh hope that Millie was still somewhere out there, alive.

His attention returned to the scowling marquess. "Lord Westbrook, I have some questions for you. If we could speak somewhere private?"

The man's reaction leaped from surprise to insult to aggression, all before replying, "Questions in regard to what?"

Rather than enter into it here, with so many others looking on, Hugh turned to the duke. "Can we make use of your study?"

Fournier peered at Hugh with slightly less hostility than Westbrook's. Though surely, he wasn't happy that one of his guests was being singled out. "As this is my home, I insist on attending the meeting."

"I've no objection to that," Hugh replied. In fact, it would be best to have the duke present. With his even temper, he may well help keep Westbrook in line.

"I will also attend." Audrey stepped forward, away from Genie and Cassandra.

Westbrook scoffed. "I am sure that is not necessary, Your Grace."

"Yes, my dear, you've spent hours on the roads," Genie said with care. "Wouldn't you like to freshen yourself before dinner?"

Audrey had relinquished her hat and gloves and spencer to her maid for cleaning, but the dust had also coated her cheeks and forehead, as well as her skirt. Any other lady might have insisted on bathing and a rest before allowing anyone to lay eyes upon her; Audrey, however, looked ready to do battle with Lord Westbrook—or with anyone who dared tell her she could not attend the questioning.

"I'm sure Greer is already drawing a bath," Audrey replied to her sister-in-law. "However, it will have to wait. I have questions for Lord Westbrook."

The man emitted a croaking noise as he gaped at her. "I hardly think you have questions that His Grace and Lord Neatham cannot ask in your stead. This is a business for men, I am sure."

Insult and ire flared in Audrey's eyes, and though it would have been entertaining to hear her give the marquess a proper dressing down, Hugh's patience had depleted.

"The dowager duchess will join us whether you think it necessary or not, Lord Westbrook." His tone brooked no argument. The marquess buttoned his lips, and Fournier gestured for Westbrook, now purpling around his cravat, to follow. They both turned toward the stairs.

Audrey fell into step beside Hugh. "He is insufferable," she whispered when the two other men were well ahead.

"He's everything I despise in men of his ilk. Pompous, entitled, superior," Hugh replied. And Westbrook wasn't artful in the least about disguising his snobbishness. Instead, he wore it on his sleeve, like a badge of honor.

"I wonder at his presence for this house party," Audrey said. "Do you think that Millie might have been coming to Greenbriar to meet with him for some reason?"

"Possibly. But I can't grasp the connection between them. He seems to have no opinion at all of your sister." Westbrook's reticence to display any concern for Lady Redding's predicament did not fit that of a man intending to propose.

"Is there any point in asking you to let me do the talking?" Hugh said as they approached the doors to the duke's study. Audrey scowled at him playfully.

"None at all."

He fought the desire to tug her aside and kiss her. "That is what I thought."

TWELVE

Michael was pouring a round of whiskies when she and Hugh entered the study. Audrey was hopeful one of the glasses was meant for her, but knowing her brother-in-law, she wouldn't count on it. For a moment, she debated on joining him at the decanters and pouring her own, if only to fortify herself for the coming conversation. Lord Westbrook's surly reaction to being questioned hadn't been remarkable. In fact, his agitation only indicated that he was hiding something.

The marquess stood stiffly, his whole demeanor radiating indignance.

"Ask your questions, then, though I don't know what the devil this could be about," he all but shouted.

The whisky would have to come later. Getting this interview finished was far more appealing. She remained standing, her hands resting on the back of a leather club chair.

"This is about your intention to propose to Lady Redding and your failure to react appropriately when her carriage was attacked. I want to know why."

A fleeting expression of blank mystification slackened Lord Westbrook's face before his pale skin began to redden.

"That is...utterly untrue. Absurd! Upon my word, Your Grace, I have no interest in marrying Lady Redding."

"Then why would the Baron Edgerton and Lady Edgerton be under the impression that you do?" Hugh asked.

The marquess's unvarnished confusion returned as he glared at Hugh. "I have no idea why they would be under such faulty impressions! I have never spoken to either of them about Lady Redding."

Westbrook's attention flicked back toward Audrey, who noted the blood rushing up from under his cravat to color his cheeks and the tips of his ears. Was it embarrassment or aggravation? She came around the club chair. "But you *have* spoken to someone about it, for my mother and uncle heard rumors of your plans to propose."

Michael extended a glass of whisky to Westbrook, one eyebrow pressed low in the expression he usually reserved for concern. But the marquess waved the glass away.

"They heard incorrectly, Your Grace," he said, his pique cooling, if only to a slight degree.

Audrey glanced toward Hugh, wishing she could know how he was finding the marquess's answers. Hugh had mentioned before that people often showcased the truth in the way they physically expressed themselves, rather than by what they said. She supposed she would have to wait until later to ask him whether he thought Westbrook was being duplicitous. Her own opinion was that he was telling at least a half-truth. So, what more was he not divulging?

Michael extended the rejected whisky to Hugh. He

accepted it, and his eyes met Audrey's as he put the glass to his lips. Though Hugh was the one sipping the whisky, her insides warmed as if she'd just sipped the spirits too. The day's ride to Kent had been awkward, to say the least. With Greer between them, Audrey had been at a complete loss for conversation. What else was there to speak of other than Millie's case, which they had no new information to examine, or their night together? They had only spent a handful of hours alone in her bedroom, but to Audrey it felt as if the whole world had shifted in that short amount of time.

He loved her. Wanted to marry her. Of course, she had hoped for these things but to hear him say them had been unexpectedly emotional. Rarely did Hugh show his vulnerabilities, but that morning as the sun rose, he'd been undressed in more than one way. He'd brought her closer to him. Made himself a part of her, and her of him.

She'd wanted time itself to stop and allow them to stay there forever. But her sister's safety, and the mystery surrounding her abduction, could not be ignored once the sun was up. There would be time for her and Hugh again; Millie, however, might not have much time left.

"How does any of this concern the lady's disappearance?" Michael asked after a short pause, allowing Lord Westbrook to calm.

"Quite right," the marquess said with a resurgence of indignation. Then, as if it had just occurred to him, "You cannot possibly think I have anything to do with this crime?"

The marquess looked like he would suffer an apoplexy if they replied that they had indeed considered it. But though he was disagreeable, Audrey wasn't convinced he was involved. Nor did the rumor her mother and uncle shared seem to have any truth to it.

"We are simply attempting to piece together why the viscountess would have been on her way to Greenbriar," Hugh said before Audrey could part her lips. She shot him an aggrieved glance.

"It was not to rendezvous with me, I can assure you of that." Westbrook smoothed his waistcoat, then checked his fob watch. "Now, if that is all? I would like to prepare for dinner."

Hugh held out an arm, gesturing that he was free to leave. Westbrook did, though not without another insouciant sniff.

Once he'd left, Audrey let her shoulders drop and set her eyes on the whisky decanter. "I wouldn't mind a drink myself," she said, and then crossed the study to pour herself one.

Michael held his opinion but pressed down an eyebrow again. She didn't think the expression was in response to the liberal amount splashing into her glass. He'd looked at Lord Westbrook with concern earlier.

Audrey sipped, the smoky flavor expanding as it slid down her throat. "Michael, what is your opinion of Lord Westbrook?"

He sat in one of the leather club chairs, but perched near the edge. He wasn't one to relax. "He isn't a close acquaintance, but Genie suggested he be invited, as he and Kettleridge are connected."

Lord Kettleridge had seemed affable enough in the foyer when they'd returned a short while ago, but Audrey was not looking forward to meeting with his daughter, Lady Veronica. There was no doubt in her mind now as to Hugh's affections, or his intentions, but she still did not wish to meet the young debutante whose sights were set on the new Lord Neatham.

Hugh took his whisky to the window, where rain lashed the glass. "Connected how?"

"Similar politics, mostly. They share a standing game of poker every week at White's," Michael answered.

"He gambles?"

Michael chuckled. "He isn't a degenerate if that is what you're asking. Many peers play at cards."

"And many gamble away their fortunes," Hugh replied before pivoting to something he and Audrey had agreed upon earlier to share with the duke. "Now that we are alone, there is something we have learned since our visit to Haverfield. It has to do with Lord Reginald Cartwright."

Michael knew the name. "Montague's heir?"

Succinctly, Hugh and Audrey informed him of Millie and Lord Cartwright's past, the rare purple diamond, the recent letters, and the even more recent disappearance of Lord Cartwright himself. Afterward, Michael drained his glass and stood.

"This is strange indeed," he muttered, pressing down a brow again. Audrey sighed.

"What are you thinking?" she asked. "There is no point denying it—I know when something is bothering you."

He began to pace. "The first, is the fact that there has been no ransom note. No letter of demand at all, as what is usual in a kidnapping situation. Now, after hearing about Cartwright, however, I begin to feel less guilty about an earlier theory."

"What theory is that?" Audrey asked, growing alarmed. Because she thought she knew exactly where Michael's mind was heading.

"That she has left of her own accord. Perhaps something went awry, and her driver and maid were caught in some violence. But if Lady Redding was trying to escape Lord Cartwright—"

"She had no reason to escape him! All she had to do was reject him if she didn't wish to marry him," Audrey argued. "Besides, he said they had agreed to marry and to tell Lord Edgerton and my mother."

"We have no evidence of Millie's responses to Cartwright," Hugh reminded her. She sealed her lips and seared him with a glare.

"Except the obvious fact that she read his letters so much she wore the paper thin with her fingers," she pointed out.

Hugh held up his hands in surrender. "I'm not saying I don't believe Cartwright. But your sister did hide his letters and lied to her staff that she was on her way to Haverfield when she came in this direction instead. She was keeping a secret."

A secret her maid, Celine, had betrayed, according to the vision Audrey had while holding the cross pendant.

"But beyond that theory, which I admit is thin," Michael went on, severing Audrey's glare at Hugh, "a second concern revolves around a Montague connection. It could be nothing, but after the two of you left for Reddingate, Kettleridge arrived. He and Westbrook began discussing a speculation. Silver mining in Brazil."

Hugh groaned. "Speculation. Yet another way to gamble away a fortune."

This time, Michael didn't refute Hugh's skepticism. "I've no appetite for it myself, but Kettleridge and Westbrook are certainly game. They're hoping to find more investors in the coming weeks. I've told all my guests to be on their guard," he added with a none-too-serious grin.

Wealthy men were often invited to pour their money into one venture or another, on the hope that their returns would far surpass their investment. The other day, as Audrey was about to leave Greenbriar, Genie said that there would be much talk of business among the men for the next fortnight.

"Are you concerned about this speculation?" she asked Michael.

He shook his head. "Not that. It's a comment Westbrook made. That perhaps they should invite wealthy widows to buy shares."

"Did he mention Lady Redding?" Hugh asked.

"Not by name, but Kettleridge has let on that Westbrook is less than flush since a bad investment last year. An import of Indian silk, I think it was. The ship sunk and the cargo was lost."

Connecting threads strummed through Audrey. Cartwright had been in India until recently.

"An East India ship?" Hugh asked, clearly making the same connection.

"Not that I'm aware. Westbrook didn't like the idea of inviting widows to partake in Henley's speculation, but it's common knowledge that Lady Redding was left a significant fortune. And that she has yet to remarry."

Another thread pulled taut in Audrey mind. "Henley, did you say?"

"Yes, this whole thing is Mr. Henley's venture."

"And Mr. Robert Henley is Montague's other grandson." Audrey recalled the man's name from their conversation with Lord Cartwright the day before, when speaking at her family plot.

Hugh came back from the window, his interest sharpened. "Is Mr. Henley one of your guests?"

"No, he gave his regrets," he replied as he started toward the study door. "But it is a strange coincidence, is it not, that Cartwright should turn up after all these years just as Henley is putting together this venture."

Without saying it outright, Michael was suggesting Lord Cartwright had only come back to Millie now because of her fortune, and her potential investing power. However, Lord Cartwright had said he'd made his own fortune in India. Again, that was just his claim. Whether it was true or not remained unknown.

"I never trust coincidences," Hugh said darkly.

Michael only crinkled his brow, as if in agreement. "I will see you at dinner," he said, then departed.

The mantel clock showed the hour nearing toward seven. Audrey did need to bathe before joining the others, and she also needed some time to pick apart and then piece together everything Michael had imparted. One piece, however, finally began to make sense.

Audrey set down her glass, unable to finish her whisky, and turned to Hugh.

"A rare purple diamond is sure to provide someone a hefty amount of money to invest."

Hugh picked up her glass and with one toss, finished the rest of her drink. "My money's back on Westbrook. If his estate is in trouble, he'd benefit from that ring. Perhaps he hired men and things went all wrong. His under-reaction to everything that's happened could be an act to appear innocent."

"But how could he have known about it? Or that Millie would be on the road to Greenbriar?"

Hugh shook his head, no answer to give. The only sound now was the rain whipping the glass windows. Hugh reached for Audrey's hand and brought it to his lips. She wanted to rise to her toes and kiss him, but if someone walked into the study, the flagrant offense would make its way around to the other guests, then to London and polite society at large.

She settled for holding his hand and a rather unsophisticated moment of longing.

"I don't imagine I'll be seated next to you at dinner," he said.

"With hope, I'll be placed next to Lord Kettleridge," she replied, suddenly no longer dreading dinner or the other guests. Hugh cocked his head.

"Why is that?"

"I hear they are looking for wealthy widows to invest in this silver speculation." She enjoyed the perceptive grin spreading over his mouth. "And I just happen to be one."

THIRTEEN

I n the two days Hugh had been gone from Greenbriar, Basil had arranged everything in his guest room with his usual exacting precision. The valet had organized all his clothing by purpose—riding, dining, lounging, boating, shooting—with several options for each. Every neckcloth was perfectly starched, his footwear polished to a high gleam, and his hats and coats brushed with the loving care of a snobby perfectionist.

"You look no better than a dog after it has rolled around in the dirt to rid itself of fleas," Basil had muttered while impatiently waiting for Hugh to remove his clothing.

"It is road dust, Basil. Forgive me if I am not some magical being that can deflect all dirt and debris."

He'd plunged into the waiting bath and summarily dismissed his fastidious valet when he'd tried scrubbing the back of Hugh's neck. The man had been a fusspot when Hugh had first hired him, and he'd only gotten worse. Now, as valet to a viscount, he was next to impossible. Though Hugh threatened to replace him on a near daily basis, Basil confidently ignored him, and with good reason. The truth was, Hugh did not implicitly trust many people. As irritating as Basil could be, he was one of the scarce few he knew he could depend upon. He was also an incurable gossip, which often came in useful.

"Have you met Westbrook's valet while I've been away?" Hugh asked him now as he tied his cravat. They stood in his dressing room, Basil readying him for dinner. Thornton, already presentable, though with a slightly rakish loose cravat that could have used a bit more starch, lounged on a quilted divan with his face stuck in a book. By the looks of it, a medical text. Seated on a cushioned stool near the open window, Sir was busy whittling a knob of wood with a folding knife.

"I have," Basil replied. "The fellow has far too heavy a hand with the pomade, if you ask me. His lordship appears as if he's been caught in a downpour."

Thornton snorted laughter before turning a page in his book.

"The state of Westbrook's hair isn't my concern," Hugh said. "I'm more curious if his valet is loose lipped about his employer."

"Granger's his name, and he's a right idiot, that one," Sir said, brushing some carvings from his hand. The boy perked up. "I could get him talkin' real easy. You got something for me to do, Lord Hugh? What you want to know?"

"His lordship doesn't need you nattering on to the marquess's help," Basil replied. "I am more than capable of speaking to the man without appearing obvious. I've already had a few conversations with him."

"Yeah, about boot black and macassar oil," Sir groaned.

"Give me something to do, Lord Hugh, I'm beggin' ya. I'm dead bored! Look at me—I'm so bored, I've had to take up whittling." Sir brandished his carving.

Thornton lowered his book. "What is that supposed to be anyhow, Sir? A cat?"

Sir glowered at the knob of wood, which did appear to be some sort of hunched animal. "A cat? This here's a horse!"

Thornton merely raised his book again, obscuring his amusement. Sir pocketed the knife and wood and crossed his arms with a huff.

"As much as I dislike agreeing with our young assistant—"

"I ain't *your* assistant, Baz."

"—it is true that Granger isn't overly cautious with details pertaining to his lordship."

"What sort of details?" Hugh asked as Basil finished with the cravat and stepped back to inspect his work. With a press of his lips, he sighed and came back again to fix something that likely did not need fixing.

"He has made a few slips, revealing the marquess is not as plump in the purse as he once was. He was quite distressed that a few articles of clothing were held over from last season, and that he was forced to economize. He also lamented about purchasing a substandard bottle of macassar oil. Of course, if he simply applied less..." Basil sighed and left the comment unfinished.

So, Westbrook's need for money might be dire. Buying into this silver venture could benefit him greatly. As would marrying Lady Redding, should she accept. Although, how would Westbrook even know of the ring, let alone that it was with Lady Redding? According to Cartwright no one knew he'd given the ring to her...except for possibly his valet.

As Basil hummed under his breath and re-pinned the cravat, Hugh's mind shifted course.

"Say a man is divested from his valet," he said. "Where would the valet go?"

Basil cut him a flat glare. "Your threats are becoming tedious."

"I am not speaking of you this time. Answer the question."

"Divested how?" Thornton asked.

"For instance, if he has a falling out with his family and leaves the household, not taking anyone or anything with him."

Basil now observed his finished cravat knot with satisfaction. Turning to clean up the dressing room, he said, "I suppose he might be shuffled off to another male in the family who doesn't already possess a servant, or who is unhappy with his current one. Thankfully, I have never been in that predicament. It is hardly enviable, for either party. Does this have to do with Granger?"

"No," Hugh said, avoiding a look in the mirror for fear of laughing at his stuffy reflection. Basil adored a tight cravat knot, but as soon as he could, Hugh would loosen it to appear more like Thornton's. "Do you know anything at all of Mr. Robert Henley? If he perhaps has a valet?"

Basil frowned as he removed the dinner jacket that had been hanging on the dressboy. "I'm not familiar with a Mr. Robert Henley."

Sir perked again. "Is he a guest? I could nick into his room and do some snooping."

"Unfortunately, he's not. He was invited but couldn't attend." Hugh slid his arms into the dinner jacket and then submitted himself to more brushing and inspecting of the black superfine.

Thornton laid his book flat on his chest. "You're thinking Cartwright's former valet went to his cousin."

"Perhaps." Cartwright had, after all, mentioned their grandfather preferred Henley. "I'd like to find out."

With a leap, Sir launched himself from the stool and grabbed his hat. "Finally, something interesting to do." He darted from the dressing room and out of sight.

"Good, that will keep him busy and away from any unsuspecting blocks of wood," Thornton said, folding his book and rising from the divan.

"I am only grateful the boy was whittling and not practicing his aim with that wretched slingshot," Basil said, then glanced at Thornton with an exasperated sigh.

As soon as he left the room, Hugh tugged the cravat choking him. "I can hardly believe it—Basil resisted commenting on the creases you've just put in your jacket by lying around."

"Baz is a treasure," Thornton said, still sitting.

"Cartwright said his valet might have known about the ring going to Lady Redding, and if now that same valet is Mr. Henley's...and Henley is running this investment venture...one that Westbrook needed a good chunk of funds to join..." But the threads began to cross, then tangle, and Hugh abandoned speaking. It made no sense aloud, but his gut still insisted there was something there.

He tugged on the cuffs of his dinner jacket and then stuck a finger down his cravat to pull some more.

"Something is different with you," Thornton said.

Hugh peered at his friend, ready to laugh at the strange remark. But then he realized what Thornton must have perceived. They were as close as brothers, and Grant Thornton was eerily observant. If he had not already elected to send his father, the Marquess of Lindstrom into a fit of fury by entering the medical profession, he would have been just as effective as a Bow Street Runner.

Hugh looked away and into the mirror, pretending to care about the state of his neckcloth.

"Is it what I think it is?" Thornton pressed.

"I cannot read your mind."

"You spent the night with her."

The comment riled him unreasonably, and he couldn't tamp it down. Hugh turned from the mirror to face his friend. "We are not discussing this."

It only spurred Thornton on. He let out a low whistle. "You've never been secretive about your liaisons before."

Hugh gritted his teeth and exhaled, trying to calm. Like a brother, Thornton enjoyed teasing. And Hugh would give it right back, in spades. However, nothing about Audrey was a lark.

"This is different," he replied. Then, holding Thornton's stare in the mirror's reflection, he added, "There will be no one else from now on."

The boyish humor vanished from the physician's expression, replaced by a genuine smile, still boyish but in no way mischievous. "It's about damn time. I am happy for you, truly." Thornton's bright smile grew fainter for a moment before he cleared his throat and got to his feet.

"I will leave you to your pining and see you at dinner," he

said, pretending that he had not just been thinking about his dead wife. "Not to worry, I know better than to say anything to anyone, especially since the lady in question is in mourning."

"Decent of you," Hugh said, absorbing a strike of contrition. Though he told his friend nearly everything, he could not reveal the truth about Philip. Sharing the burden with Audrey didn't bother him, though. They were in this together.

———

With the deluge of rain and wind, the dining room windows were only open a mere inch to avoid blustery wet gales from whipping inside. In turn, the air in the large room grew stuffy and humid almost immediately after everyone took their seats. To make matters worse, Hugh had been placed next to Lady Veronica on his left, and her mother, Lady Kettleridge, on his right.

There were a dozen people seated at the long table. He'd been introduced to the other guests before dinner, when gathering in the drawing room, but most of them Hugh did not know, nor did he care to. The only person he was interested in was not an official guest at all.

"My sister-in-law, the dowager duchess, will be joining our party for the time being," Genie had said, welcoming Audrey as she entered the drawing room in her simple, unadorned widow's black.

No one had breathed a word of the events involving the two killings and Lady Redding, though every guest had learned of it by now. For Lady Kettleridge, though, the circumstances weren't extraordinary enough to convince her of Audrey's need to remain.

"Sir Ridley and His Grace have everything in hand. As do you, Lord Neatham, to be sure," the woman fawned in between dainty bites of her salmon pate. "I simply don't understand what the dowager can hope to accomplish by staying at Greenbriar. It's quite out of the ordinary for a woman in mourning to be socializing like this."

They were seated far from Audrey, and with any hope, the murmurs of conversation concealed Lady Kettleridge's voice. Then again, the woman's pitch could likely be heard by servants in the kitchens.

"I would hardly describe her as socializing," Veronica replied to her mother. Hugh had a moment of appreciation for her. It quickly wilted. "She is dejected, can't you see? Her yellow, sickly pallor is evidence of it. She would have been better served having a tray sent to her room. I can barely touch a morsel myself, she is so miserable. Do you not agree, Lord Neatham?"

Hugh pinned his lips against a laugh. Audrey's widow's black certainly stood out among the colorful gowns worn by the other ladies. An even mix of ages and society ranks, he noted. But as she turned an ear toward Mr. Filmore, a prosperous merchant with connections to Henley and his silver venture, Hugh did not think she looked miserable.

"On the contrary, she appears to be enduring a difficult situation with admirable grace," he replied, lifting his glass of wine.

"Your charitable words do you credit, my lord," Lady Kettleridge said, leaning toward his arm. He resisted the urge to sit back.

"Indeed," Veronica murmured.

Her glossy chestnut hair, heart-shaped face, and dark brown eyes fringed with thick lashes secured her beauty, but it was her mouth that Hugh imagined men would find the most tempting. Wide and generous, her lips curved into a perfect cupid's bow. She employed those lips to their fullest effect right then, aware that they were a prime asset.

"Her Grace is fortunate to have your expertise in the matter. She has endured so much lately. This tragedy direct on the heels of the one that stole away her husband. It is terribly unfair. And to not have any children to take comfort in," she said with a sad shake of her head. Then, as if rallying, "But that is not her fault, is it? It is nature's way, and who are we to judge?"

Lady Kettleridge made a nod of agreement, and Hugh attempted to let the comment pass. Veronica, along with the rest of society, was under the impression that Audrey was barren. With no heir after the nearly four years her marriage had lasted, it was the obvious deduction.

He glanced down the table and caught Audrey looking at him. She averted her eyes quickly. He'd also caught her assessing Veronica during the soup course, and then again during the salad and cheese course. Rumors of his interest in the debutante had brought out an unexpected envy in her, but surely now she could trust his devotion to her was firm?

"I know you did not wish to say earlier in the drawing room when everyone hounded you with questions, but as we have grown so close, my lord, do tell us—have you narrowed in on a suspect in the case of the murders and disappearance?" Lady Kettleridge asked with the same fervor the other guests had shown before dinner. He had stayed close-lipped then and didn't plan to divulge anything now either.

"We are making strides," he replied vaguely.

"We?" Veronica said. "You do not refer to the dowager duchess, I hope?"

He took another bracing gulp of wine and after swallowing answered, "That is who I refer to, yes. Her Grace has proved to have a keen mind when it comes to matters like these."

This left the two ladies speechless for a moment. Then, Lady Kettleridge twittered and tapped him on the forearm. "Oh! How you make me laugh, my lord!"

Veronica, however, did not follow her mother's exuberant reaction. "How curious that Her Grace has had the misfortune to be involved in quite a few predicaments requiring your assistance." The young lady's eyes shifted smoothly to view the other end of the table, where the topic of their conversation sat, politely listening to Mr. Filmore. Veronica's veiled accusation—that Audrey was somehow fabricating trouble simply to find a reason to be at his side— was as tedious as it was ludicrous.

He found he couldn't formulate a reply that would not bite as severely as Veronica just had while glaring at Audrey. He hadn't seen it before while dining with the lady and her family at Sir Gabriel's, but he did now: Lord Kettleridge's intent to betroth his daughter to Hugh was clearly not just *Kettleridge's* objective.

He sighed. He would need to speak plainly to the man.

"I do hope this rain clears," Lady Kettleridge said a few moments later after an awkward pause. "Your Grace," she called to their hostess, at the head of the table. "You will still hold the regatta tomorrow if the rain dries, I hope?"

"Yes, of course," Genie replied with a cautious glance toward Audrey and Fournier. "We must continue on for now, I think. It would be good sport."

"For the ladies and gentlemen alike," Cassandra said, pinning the duke with an expectant glare. "Isn't that right, brother?"

Fournier looked far from happy, but he merely grunted agreement. "The ladies may row as well."

Hugh had been ignoring Westbrook, who had thankfully been seated well away from Audrey. But now, the marquess huffed his disapproval. "Next they'll be joining us for the shooting."

"Excellent suggestion, my lord," Cassandra said brightly. "I am a rather good shot, as are many ladies. Mrs. Filmore, I hear you took down a stag last autumn."

Mr. Filmore's wife sipped her wine while looking sideways at Westbrook. "It was a wild boar, my dear."

Thornton smirked and shared a conspiratorial grin with Cassie at his side. But her humor quickly faded when another young woman, seated across the table from Hugh, spoke up.

"I do love a fox hunt," Miss Cynthia Stewart said brightly. "My father would allow me to tag along whenever he ran the hounds at our estate in Derbyshire."

Mrs. Stewart added softly, "God rest his soul."

Earlier in the drawing room, Hugh had learned the Stewarts had been neighbors and friends of Genie's family. The younger son of a viscount, Mr. Stewart had taken ill the previous autumn and passed on before Miss Cynthia, his sole daughter, could make her debut during the season. The gleam of interest in Mrs. Stewart's eyes when Genie had introduced Cynthia to Hugh had been as cunning as Lady Kettleridge's and had left him just as discomfited.

Cassie pressed her lips thin and made a show of looking down the table, away from Cynthia. Three debutantes might have been too many for one house party, Hugh thought, but at least with Cassie, he knew she had no designs on him.

"Well then, I shall take part in the regatta," Veronica said at a pitch loud enough for the whole dinner party to hear. "I am no wilting violet and have some experience boating. What do you say, Lord Neatham, to my joining your crew?"

Rowing in a regatta across Greenbriar's lake did not appeal to him in the least, especially when there was a missing viscountess to track down. While the murder investigation was now in the hands of the magistrate, Sir Ridley, and the man would surely like to find Lady Redding too, it was Hugh and Audrey who had leads to follow. But asking to row on his crew in front of all and sundry had been a well-played move. He could not refuse her without appearing unspeakably rude.

He grinned stiffly and hoped it did not appear as forced as it felt. "I would be delighted."

CHAPTER

FOURTEEN

M r. Filmore, seated to Audrey's left, should have occupied her interest vastly more than the debutante several chairs down the long, crystal- and china-filled table. Unfortunately, she found it difficult to focus on the forty-something member of the landed gentry when the young and beautiful Lady Veronica continued to simper at Hugh.

Necessity forced her hand, however. With a simple prompt, asking whether he had any knowledge of the silver venture, Mr. Filmore had spilled forth with a veritable tide of information, all of which she heard and committed to memory. He had accumulated great wealth through shipping and trade and was now investing in steam engines and, as of several months ago, in the Brazilian silver mine.

As interested as she was in Mr. Filmore's knowledge, she couldn't help but wish that Genie had seated Hugh closer to them so that he could take part in the conversation too. Instead, he sat at the other end of the table, cradled between Lady Kettleridge and the delectable Lady Veronica. She had made her bow the previous Season, and it was said she'd received numerous offers, but none that had matched what she or her father, the Earl of Kettleridge, expected in the man who would win her hand. With an exorbitant dowry and a face to rival Helen of Troy—or so the gossip sheets had printed—Lady Veronica was the catch of the Season. And she had her sights firmly set on the new Lord Neatham.

"*Five. Thousand. Pounds.*"

Audrey cut her eyes away from Hugh and Veronica and focused again on Mr. Filmore. He'd formed the number with elaborate pauses to indicate the weight of the sum.

"I'm sorry?" she said, having forgotten her initial question before Mr. Filmore had gone on a meandering explanation of the demand of silver, most of which she had not paid attention to. But then, she remembered.

"Oh, yes, of course. The initial investment. Five thousand?" The steep amount now made an impact. "That is quite dear."

"It is, indeed," he said. "But it takes money to make money, as my father always intoned, and he steered me well in my earlier investments."

During the last few courses as Mr. Filmore had discussed his business in investing and in the silver mine specifically, Audrey had gotten the sense that the man was not conceited about his wealth so much as he was exuberant. He was energetic in his conversation and did not seem to acknowledge the startled reception of it among those around him. He was the sort of man to lean a hair too close when speaking, though not in any threatening way. Mr. Filmore was simply animated.

"Tell me, Mr. Filmore, did many other men such as your-self join with Mr. Henley in his venture?"

At her right, she sensed rather than saw Lord Thornton's interest; he and Cassie had been making polite conversation, but it appeared to have stalled.

"Several," he replied. "When he brought Mr. Teague, the owner of the mine, to White's, he turned heads, indeed. Mr. Teague is a most amiable fellow. No matter that he is not a peer. Fine business sense and a penchant for adventure saw him flush with more wealth than he knew what to do with."

Beside her, Thornton turned to enter the conversation. "I have not heard of this Mr. Teague. Does he hail from London?"

"Trinidad. Owns a few estates there. Sugar, you know. A trip to Brazil and a chance meeting with a local tribal elder or some such, and he discovered a lode of silver, ripe for mining."

"I do hope this Mr. Teague is fairly compensating the villagers there," Audrey said, her stomach curling at the thought that this man could have simply waltzed in and taken what the locals had not realized would be so profitable to them.

By Mr. Filmore's blank expression, she presumed he had not thought about that aspect just yet. Audrey sighed and moved on, though not without first glancing toward Hugh and Lady Veronica again; she and her mother had leaned forward to confer over Hugh's plate. Veronica's insistence that she join his regatta crew the following day had brought on an uninvited surge of envy, which she had been trying to temper. How absurd! Hugh had declared himself to her. There was no reason to be jealous of Lady Veronica Langton.

"How might one participate in this venture?" Cassie asked, leaning forward to peer around Lord Thornton's broad shoulders.

Mr. Filmore smiled widely at her inquiry, though with a hint of discomfort. "I am afraid it is not customary for the female sex to enter into such business partnerships."

"Why ever not?" Cassie demanded. "If she has the funds to buy in, what does it matter whether the investor wears a gown or a pair of trousers?"

It was the perfect segue for Audrey, and it had not even been planned. She silently thanked her sister-in-law. "Yes, Mr. Filmore, I find I agree. And furthermore, might someone buy shares in this venture with only bank notes, or would other items of value be permissible? Unentailed land, perhaps...or say, jewels?"

Mr. Filmore laughed gaily. "Oh, no, no. Property or gemstones would not be acceptable. Pounds sterling, that is all that will do for something of this magnitude. You see, that is why it is best to leave men to these things, Your Grace, my lady. They are better equipped for such endeavors," he said, though not as condescendingly as Lord Westbrook might have done so. Mr. Filmore was too jovial to come off as purposefully arrogant.

"Yes, ladies, do remember your places," Thornton murmured, his sarcasm betrayed only by the barest twitch of his lower lip. Cassie's heated glare seared him, his mockery of Mr. Filmore's lecture lost on her.

Audrey pondered what Mr. Filmore had said; even if someone had wanted the purple diamond to buy into this venture, he could not do so with the ring itself. He would first need to fence it. There were any number of pawnbrokers in London, but with a jewel so noticeable, that would be quite the risk. Scotland, however, had its fair share of shops that would turn a blind eye to possibly stolen goods along the borderlands.

"I am disappointed that Mr. Henley gave his regrets to our hosts. Kettleridge, Westbrook, and I are eager to hear about the first quarter returns," Mr. Filmore went on.

While this captured Audrey's attention, Cassie was still focused on what Lord Thornton had quipped. "I'll have you know, that once I reach my majority, I plan to invest a good portion of my dowry."

The physician looked askance at her. "Is your dowry not set aside for your future husband?"

Cassie hitched her chin. "I do not plan to marry." She then sealed her lips, picked up her spoon, and speared the pudding on her plate.

Audrey momentarily forgot her objective with Mr. Filmore and peered around Lord Thornton's shoulder at her sister-in-law.

"Forgive me," the physician said, appearing contrite. "I had heard a rumor that is apparently baseless."

Since the spring, Cassie had been courting Mr. William Knowlton—Genie's youngest brother, a handsome and affable fellow recently out of university. It was a well-known connection, and there had been whisperings around society, and even printed in the gossip columns, that a betrothal was forthcoming.

After Cassie's distressing last year, Audrey had been pleased to see her in the first stages of falling in love. She couldn't ask questions here, in front of everyone, but would certainly do so later.

However, Cassie's brother Tobias held no such reservations. Seated directly across the table, and apparently having ignored the conversation on his side in favor of theirs, he snorted in derision. "She is better off without the cad."

Cassie glared. "Quiet, Toby." She checked the head of the table where Genie sat, thankfully oblivious to them. Pink flooded Cassie's cheeks. Thornton raised a brow, but Cassie pointedly avoided him by shifting in her seat to turn and speak to the man on her right.

By then, Mr. Filmore was in conversation with his other neighbor, and everyone was nearly finished with their dessert course anyhow. The men were to withdraw to the billiards room for cigars and port, and the ladies to Genie's drawing room for cards and sherry. The idea of joining them made Audrey wilt; and not only because she would be made to converse with Lady Veronica—something she had avoided thus far. She had not been alone for days, and she yearned for a short stretch of time to sit and think. So, as the other ladies filed out of the dining room, Audrey touched Cassie's arm and told her to pass along to Genie that she would retiring for the night.

Then, she started for the library. Greer would be in the bedchamber, preparing for her nightly ablutions, but even though her maid was unobtrusive, Audrey needed solitude. So, she made her way up into the mezzanine of the library, directly into the alcove she had come to prefer over the last two months at Greenbriar.

The thunderstorm had let up a little, and a mild rain flecked the round window. She lit a lamp and, removing her slippers, sat into the armchair and tucked her feet under her. Closing her eyes, she tried to relax and make her mind go blank, but it refused. Instead, it pored over everything Mr. Filmore had said about the investment venture.

Why had Mr. Henley changed his mind about attending the house party with such short notice? His connection to Lord Cartwright and thus, Millie, also bothered her...there was something there. Frustration brimming, Audrey rubbed her temple, stymied. Every moment she could not determine who took Millie and why, was another moment her sister's life was imperiled.

What use was her gift of being able to see the clues other people could not, if she still failed to make sense of them?

She and Philip used to argue about whether her ability was a gift or a curse. While Audrey often bounced between finding it to be one or the other, Philip had always firmly seen it at worst, as a curse and at best, a lonely gift. *It is an experience you can never share with any other person. You alone can see the things you do,* he'd once said to her when she asked him what he meant by it being a lonely gift. *You have something other people can't comprehend, and it sets you apart from them.*

He hadn't been trying to be callous; he was only ever blunt. He'd been correct, too. There was something incredibly lonely about not being able to share the knowledge she was given. Though, she'd been able to at least talk about it with Philip, and now with Hugh.

With no one nearby to observe her, she could let the wide, giddy grin she'd been suppressing to finally form. The memories of last night were so vivid, she could almost feel the pressure of his hands, his mouth, his body, against hers. So much had changed, so many doubts laid to rest.

Lolling her head to the side, she noticed a thick tome

open on the table next to her chair; it seemed Audrey was not the only guest who had discovered this reading alcove. Shifting the book to view the spine, *Country Estates of the British Peerage*, she reached over and placed the attached red ribbon into the seam to mark the guest's page. It was the listing for Greenbiar. A guest had been reading up on this particular estate, curious to its history and offerings. The description logged everything from acreage and numbers of stocked ponds and gardens to the style of the home, the number of rooms, and the brief histories of past residents.

There would be a listing for Fournier Downs too, she presumed. And of Hugh's estate in Surrey, Cranleigh Manor. She hesitated before taking the tome into her lap. It still didn't feel entirely real what he'd said the previous night. That he intended to make her his wife. If she were to become Viscountess Neatham...well then, Cranleigh Manor would be her country estate, not Fournier Downs. It was such an outlandish idea that it nearly felt dreamlike.

Audrey didn't want to get ahead of herself, but she *was* alone. No one would have to know that she had read the listing for the Neatham country seat. She began to flip pages backward, assuming the listings would be alphabetical, but it soon became apparent that they were listed according to county. She was flipping back through the Kent estates when a listing stopped her: Montague Lodge. In Kent? Quickly, she read over the listing. Lord Montague's country seat was a grandiose hunting lodge in Pyke-on-Wending.

"Pyke-on-Wending," she murmured, tapping her finger against the page.

A board creaked underfoot just beyond the alcove. She

closed the heavy book just as a figure came into view at the edge of the bookshelves. She startled and froze into place.

"Lord Westbrook?"

Rather than pull back and apologize for coming upon her, the marquess remained. He wasn't surprised at all to find her. He'd clearly expected it.

Audrey set the book back onto the table and lowered her feet—free of her slippers—to the floor. He noted the state of her stockinged feet and cleared his throat.

"Your Grace." He made a short bow of his head. "Forgive me for searching you out like this. I must admit that I applied to a footman to tell me in which direction you had gone after dinner."

The sensation of her blood slowing even as her pulse began to quicken made her lightheaded as she stood from the chair.

"If this is about earlier, in the duke's study—"

"No." He took a step forward. The small area of the alcove would not permit another step without coming into her space. "Well, yes, in fact. I wished to explain."

His bearing was poles apart from his earlier indignance. Contrite seemed the best word to describe it now.

"Explain what, my lord?"

Had she been a debutante, this would be tantamount to an indecent scandal. Should they be discovered, they would be expected to marry to avoid any ruination on the lady's part. However, widows weren't subjected to such ridiculous rules.

Still, his presence unnerved her.

"My behavior. You see, I don't wish to appear unconcerned for your sister's safety, and if I came across as surly and rude earlier, please understand, it was all owing to that rumor your mother and uncle intimated to you. It took me by surprise."

"As it did me," she said. "I hope you can understand why Lord Neatham and I were perplexed by your failure to say anything at all of your intentions when Millie went missing. But if you say you don't wish for her hand..." She didn't know whether to believe him or not, and she knew Hugh was still suspicious.

"I do not," he said firmly, then took yet another step closer. Audrey pressed back, but now had nowhere to go, except back down into the armchair. She managed to stay on her feet.

"I had not planned to say anything until much later on in your mourning, of course, but I feel I ought to clear the air and make you aware. You are, after all, no blushing debutante." Audrey's palms began to sweat as she finally grasped his intent. *Oh, good heavens.* This was not what she'd expected at all.

"Your Grace, allow me to say that—"

"I thought I heard voices."

Her heart re-started at Hugh's deep timbre cutting off the marquess. He appeared in the alcove opening. Audrey was so relieved she let out an involuntary exhalation of air.

Westbrook turned and met the hard cast of Hugh's expression.

"Neatham. If you do not mind, I was speaking privately with Her Grace." The marquess clipped his words, his outrage over the intrusion evident.

However, it was Hugh, remaining silent for several moments, who chilled the small space. Had it been possible, his unyielding glare would have sealed Westbrook into a block of permafrost. Audrey had seen him annoyed before. She'd seen him angry. However, she'd never seen Hugh like this—practically luminescent in his wrath.

He took the few strides necessary to come between West-brook and Audrey, his motions dangerously calm. "I find I do mind, Westbrook. There can be no need for you to have followed her here."

As the marquess and Hugh maintained their heated glaring match, a tacit understanding seemed to pass between them.

Audrey tried to ease the tension. "Unless you have something more to say about my sister?"

The marquess peeled his livid glare from Hugh and sent it toward her. "I have nothing more. And I can see now that there is no need to speak to you on the other matter. Good evening."

With a curt bob of his head, he spun around and retreated from the alcove. Audrey let out another pent-up breath, deflating. "That was excellent timing," she sighed.

Hugh remained vigilant, moving to the alcove corner, and peering out to be sure the marquess had left. "I followed him. I suspected he'd try to find you."

"Why?"

"Because your mother got it wrong. The rumor she heard had nothing to do with her eldest daughter."

Hugh finally relaxed, his intimidating glare softening with a sparkle of amusement as he faced her. Audrey groaned and covered her cheeks with the palms of her hands.

"Mother must have heard that Lord Westbrook wished to marry her widowed daughter. But he meant me, not

Millie." She shivered. "The man has been nothing but stand-offish and belittling since we met. If that is how he sets out to charm a woman, I hate to think how he would treat someone he did not wish to impress."

Hugh chuckled darkly. "I suppose, as much as I'd liked to have laid him out flat for cornering you in the very place you warned me about, he doesn't have any connection to Millie's disappearance after all."

She deflated a little more knowing that door had closed. And how few more there were left open to them.

Hugh stepped closer, and unlike when Lord Westbrook had done the same, Audrey did not want Hugh to stop. She wanted him to wrap her into his arms and kiss her again. However, he held back.

"You know, he is not the only peer with that plan."

It took a moment for her to comprehend his meaning, and when she did, she felt slightly ill.

"I hadn't considered that I'd be of interest to other men within the peerage." It was naive of her, to be sure, but it simply had not yet crossed her mind. Not with her thoughts so firmly fixed on Hugh. "Well, except for one," she added with a playful grin.

"Men like Westbrook see only that you are young, gorgeous, and wealthy." Hugh moved closer with each compliment. His hands took hers and brought them to his lips. It was true; the marquess hadn't cared one jot about her. He'd been ready to propose to a stranger. Because of her money, of course.

"On the other hand, I see a mule-headed woman who is impatient and reckless," Hugh continued. Before she could part her lips in protest, he kept on. "And who is determined, clever, and uncommonly gifted."

She shook her head, knowing he was only teasing. Partially.

"What did you learn at dinner?" he asked, still drifting his lips across her knuckles. "I saw your neighbor chatting your ear off."

"Mr. Filmore," she said, deciding to say nothing about Hugh's neighbor, Lady Veronica. She would only appear petty. "He invested heavily in the silver mine venture with Mr. Henley. He said it was a five-thousand-pound buy-in. The ring Lord Cartwright spoke of cannot be worth so much, don't you think? However, one cannot purchase shares with anything other than pounds sterling. So really, the ring is useless to anyone wanting to jump into the venture, at least until it can be exchanged at a pawnbrokers."

Hugh went to the round window and levered it open a few inches, letting in a gust of fresh, rainy air. "Now that we know she was not coming here to meet with Lord Westbrook, it can only make sense that she was coming to meet with you."

Audrey longed to drop back into the armchair in exhaustion and confusion. "But why? She sent no word ahead. I was all packed up and ready to return to Hertfordshire."

Her trunks had since been returned to her room here at Greenbriar. Who knew how much longer she would stay now?

"Maybe she did," Hugh murmured.

"Did what?"

"Send word ahead. Only it was delivered into the wrong hands."

Audrey perked. "And whoever received it knew to set the trap on the road."

Hugh ran his fingers through his hair. "We can only speculate."

Audrey threw up her arms and let out a frustrated groan. "We are no closer to finding out who took Millie and killed her driver and maid than we were a few days ago. She is in danger and here we are struggling to even understand motive."

Hugh looked like he wanted to reach for her hands again. But he held still at the window. "This silver speculation may not have anything to do with it, but the connection between Montague and Cartwright and the abductor's demands for the ring lead me to think it is the best lead for us to follow."

The book of estates on the table came back to her at the mention of Lord Montague. She picked it up and opened to the marked page for Greenbriar. "Did you know that Montague Lodge is in Pyke-on-Wending? That's just north of Moorsly."

"Where the maid washed up," he said as she flipped back to find the page she'd been looking at when Westbrook appeared. She found it again and handed it to Hugh. He read the listing, his brow pulling taut.

"I think we should pay it a visit," Audrey said.

"I would rather you stay here."

Though not a surprise, it was still infuriating.

"You cannot go alone. It could be dangerous if this is where Millie has been taken." The nearness of Lord Montague's lodge and the direction in which Celine's body had washed downstream concerned her. It was too much a coincidence to not be a possibility.

"I don't plan to go alone," Hugh said. "There are plenty of men at Greenbriar to accompany me. And you will be much safer here."

"But—"

"I will gather a group first thing in the morning." He grinned mischievously. "Sadly, it looks as if I will have to forgo the regatta."

Audrey's vexation compounded at the mention of the boat race across the lake and Lady Veronica's declaration that she would row with Hugh. She sniffed. "Your crew will surely miss you."

He tossed the compendium of country estates to the leather armchair. "I know what you are thinking."

"No, you do not."

Hugh crossed his arms but stayed a good arm's reach away. "Do not pretend you weren't monitoring my conversation with Lady Veronica over dinner."

The gall! "I was doing no such thing."

"If it puts your mind at ease, I was trying to read your lips while you and Mr. Filmore were speaking."

How did he do it? He boiled her blood one moment and then, with dizzying swiftness, turned her to putty. In those moments when he was arrogant, she could not fathom why she liked him at all; but then, when he was charming and sincere, she could not fathom staying angry. Still, her intractable stubbornness was a wall slow to crumble.

"You were so occupied with Lady Veronica and Lady Kettleridge that I didn't know you were even looking my way," she said.

"I am always looking your way."

Blast the man. She could not smother her delight and

gave up trying. Audrey clasped her hands behind her back and edged toward him.

"We are finally alone," she whispered.

"In the sinfully dangerous alcove," he concurred. But though he let his eyes rove her from crown to foot, her slippers still discarded, he did not meet her advance. To her astonishment, and slight affront, he turned and made his way to the alcove opening. A dart of concern lanced through her. Until he faced her again.

"I wasn't careful last night," he said softly. "I lost control."

She tried, but failed, to understand his meaning. When he saw her confusion, he raked his fingers through his hair, slightly flustered. Even more quietly, he said, "I don't want to get you with child, Audrey."

Understanding spiraled through her then. She couldn't breathe. Couldn't speak. A fierce blush lit her cheeks, and she felt a fool for it.

"I understand," she said, a little breathless.

"Do you?"

Now she grew irritated rather than embarrassed. "Yes, of course I do." She took a breath and tried to compose herself. "Any child now would be attributed to Philip." It was, after all, one of the primary reasons the mourning period lasted for one year—to see through the length of a pregnancy.

There was also the question of whether Hugh would be reluctant to have a child with her at all. She hated to think of it, but the threat of Philip being discovered as still alive was not something Hugh would overlook or forget. If it was ever made known that Audrey was not a widow, any child she bore with Hugh would be legally regarded as Philip's. Hugh had made it clear in the past that it was important to him that no child of his be attributed to another man. She would respect that.

But she couldn't bring herself to broach the subject now. Not when he had yet to formally offer his hand.

"It would be safer to wait." He broke into a grin. "Even though resisting you may very well kill me."

Audrey laughed, though weakly as she considered the obstacles still standing in their path.

"I will endeavor to keep you alive, my lord," she replied lightly, gathering her slippers.

"And to stay out of isolated alcoves where greedy fortune hunters can corner you?"

"That too."

He held out his arm for her to grasp and gave her a wink. It cut right through to her heart.

FIFTEEN

T he moment Audrey's mourning period ended, she vowed to collect all her widow's black into a pile and set fire to it. Not only was the color unflattering, but it was also despicably hot in the sun.

Perspiration gathered on her chest and back, and her legs were positively baking as she sat near the lake's edge. The heat was smothering. So was the company. Chairs had been set out for the ladies, to watch the preparations for the regatta. Two long boats had been moored at the dock running along the water's edge, and while the teams had been settled upon the evening before, the departure of three crew mates that morning had left the remaining men questioning if the race should be postponed altogether.

Hugh had recruited both Lord Thornton and Michael to ride with him to Pyke-on-Wending, and the three had left just after breakfast, before most of the other guests had risen from their beds. Audrey, however, had been awake and ready to greet them as they descended the main stairwell in their riding clothes.

She'd debated over donning her riding habit and simply insisting upon joining them, but knowing that Michael would pitch a fit, she'd abstained—though with great difficulty. The most important thing was that Millie be found, and whether Audrey was with them or not at the time did not matter. She trusted Hugh and Michael, and of course Lord Thornton, who had brought with him his medical bag out of precaution. Audrey was also mindful of the difficult position Genie was currently in. To be hosting a house party while a black cloud hung overhead was challenge enough. To have her mourning sister-in-law riding off in a search party, inspiring gossip, would only lead to more censure. With Genie so newly a duchess, Audrey knew this party was important to her, to set her place in society. And so far, it was off to a rocky beginning.

However, as the ladies by the lake fanned themselves and spoke of the new Viscount Neatham, Audrey decided her sister-in-law owed her a great debt for behaving herself and staying at Greenbriar.

"His transformation has been nothing short of miraculous," Lady Kettleridge exclaimed. It seemed this was the only way she said anything—with great emotion and enthusiasm. "Like changing water into wine!"

Next to her, Mrs. Filmore, who was more reserved and poised, sipped her glass of lemonade before saying, "I have heard he is looking to lease Neatham House on Kensington Square. Doesn't want it."

"Kensington Square?" Miss Cynthia Stewart echoed. "Oh, how I adore Kensington Square. I can't imagine why he would not want to live there."

"Can you truly not?" Cassie interjected, a touch harsher

than necessary. She sent Miss Stewart an incisive stare. "He can't have many fond memories of that house. And I don't think he has changed so very much," she added, coming to Hugh's stalwart defense.

Lady Veronica beat her lace fan, her steady gaze hitching on Cassie. "Ah, yes. You knew him previously when he was but a Bow Street Runner."

The other ladies glanced toward Audrey, expecting Veronica to include her as one of Hugh's earlier acquaintances. When she did not, and did not even look Audrey's way, it was purposefully done.

"Officer," Audrey said.

Veronica blinked and looked over, as if just noticing she was there. "I'm sorry?"

"Officer. He was a Bow Street *officer*. And they do not overly like to be called Runners."

A false smile stretched the young woman's pillowy lips. "Is that so? How knowledgeable of you, Your Grace."

Her mockery made Audrey wish she had not risen to her petty goading. She merely smiled in return and bowed her head, as if saying, "You're welcome."

Genie, who always seemed to know what to say to either deflect conflict or redirect sticky conversations, shifted eight-month-old George on her lap. "Fine clothes and a title can only change a man to a certain degree," the duchess said evenly as the little boy reached pudgy hands toward his mother's face. His jet ringlets and big blue eyes sent a pang of longing though Audrey.

She and Philip had agreed from the outset that they would not have a child, and when he'd more recently suggested adoption, she had been uninterested. But that did not mean she didn't want a child. As Genie spoke in support of Hugh now, Audrey recalled his comment the previous night, that he did not wish to get her with child. Had he meant just not now, or not ever?

"Lord Neatham was raised by a gentleman to be a gentleman," the duchess concluded.

Audrey smiled warmly at her diplomatic sister-in-law.

"And a handsome one at that," Lady Kettleridge said with a giggle.

Genie smiled tightly. She would not be persuaded into trivial chatter. "I am glad he has come. It's quite fortunate, in fact, given his background and the unforeseen circumstances."

Again, the ladies' attentions shifted to Audrey, where she sat on the outer edge of the circle, in a spot of shade provided by a willow tree.

"I am so very sorry about the happenings with Lady Redding," Mrs. Stewart said, her expression one of genuine concern. She wasn't as talkative as the other ladies, and her daughter, Cynthia was much the same. They both appeared content to observe and offer a comment now and again.

"Thank you," Audrey said. "Though I am certain Lord Neatham will locate her."

Hopefully, he was finding her even as she spoke.

"Yes, he is quite impressive." Veronica fanned herself languidly. "However, he does have the burden of repairing the Neatham name. His best chance for that will be to take a wife with impeccable character, one who does not have the incumbrance of past scandal herself."

It was painfully obvious of whom she was speaking.

Cassie rolled her eyes as she sipped her lemonade. Lady Kettleridge made an approving trill.

"Yes, indeed, he requires a lady who can smooth his rough edges, is that not right?"

Veronica's answering simper made her appear like a cat finding a bowl of cream.

"Oh, I think his edges aren't so very rough," Cynthia said. "He seemed perfectly charming last evening at dinner."

Cassie snorted in a most unladylike fashion. "If you think scowling is charming. He looked miserable to me."

Veronica and her mother openly glared at Cassie, while Audrey pinned the inside of her cheek to avoid laughing.

These ladies were not the only ones in the ton who were fascinated with Hugh. No doubt, the taint of his former blackguard status kindled their interests. He was unlike any of the men of their social circles. However, Audrey could now tuck away her resentment for Veronica and her ilk; there was no longer any reason for her to doubt Hugh or his feelings for her. She drained her own glass of lemonade while wearing a satisfied grin.

"It is regrettable the duke and Lords Neatham and Thornton will miss the regatta," Mrs. Filmore said. "It leaves the crews in quite the lurch."

When Audrey had met them at the base of the stairs that morning, Michael had treated the outing like a fool's errand. He had sent bailiffs and farmers all over the county in search of Millie, including to Montague Lodge in Pyke-on-Wending. The light staff there informed the inquiring bailiff that Lord Montague was not in residence this summer; he was in Lyme Regis, taking the sea air and salt water for his ailing joints and lungs. The house was empty, and no one had seen anything untoward, especially not the Viscountess Redding herself. But, unsatisfied with taking another person's word for it, Hugh had wanted another look.

"Perhaps we should postpone," Genie said with a sigh.

Mr. Flint, Michael's steward, had been recruited to stand in for the duke, and Basil for Hugh, though the valet made no attempt to mask his disdain for the task. Hugh must have forced him somehow, and the middle-aged man now stood at the docks in his usual suit and with his usual haughty grimace, flapping his hand in front of his face to bat away a fly.

"There is no call for that," Cassie said, standing from her chair. "Didn't we discuss ladies participating last night at dinner? The duke approved. As such, I volunteer."

With that, she left the ladies and made her way to the dock. Tobias saw her coming and pulled a vexed face.

"I planned to sit as coxswain," Veronica said, "but I hardly think missing three of the strongest men gives either crew much of a chance now."

Hugh's absence had surely stemmed her interest as well.

"I think the crews will be evenly weighted, and certainly one must be the victor," Audrey said, admiring her younger sister-in-law as she presented herself to the other rowers. Mr. Filmore heartily welcomed her, as did Lord Kettleridge, though the others were less keen.

"It is becoming quite sweltering," Lady Veronica said, then leaned forward, directing her comment toward Audrey. "My goodness, Your Grace, you must be feeling the heat keenly wearing all that black. Perhaps you would fare better inside?"

The woman was more insufferable than the sun. Audrey

stood up from her chair, eager to be gone, though not in the direction Veronica longed for.

"I volunteer as well," she said, stoking gasps from Lady Kettleridge and Genie.

"Are you quite certain, Audrey?" Genie said, standing up and handing her now squirming son to the nursemaid. She seemed to swoon a little, and Audrey reached for her.

"Are you unwell?"

Genie shook her head and laughed. "Just this heat. I'm feeling faint. I do worry you'll feel the same if you row."

She didn't add that a woman in mourning should not be rowing with men in a regatta to begin with. But if she could not be riding with Hugh to Montague Lodge, she refused to sit around moping.

"I'm made of heartier stuff than that," she said, then started for the dock too. Cassie grinned broadly, and with their numbers now fully restored, the men made ready to get the race underway.

However, they were disrupted once more, this time by a well-dressed man as he walked alone down the sloping lawn toward their gathering. He looked to be in his middle thirties, and with his tailored summer suit and walking stick, he also looked every inch a gentleman.

"O-ho! What fortune!" Lord Kettleridge called as he caught sight of the man. Every head turned to see the approaching visitor.

"Mr. Henley, you have come at last," Genie said, starting toward him.

Audrey's stomach seemed to turn to stone as the man smiled gaily and sketched a genteel bow. *This* was Mr. Henley?

"Please accept my most earnest apologies, Your Grace," he said as all the men started forward as well. "I am dreadfully rude arriving with no forewarning."

"Not at all," Genie said, and she sounded completely genuine. "But I confess, we had not thought to see you."

"I was saddened to give my regrets, especially after so looking forward to attending. However, much to my surprise and delight, I was able to get away from the business that had been keeping me in London." He doffed his buff-colored top hat and tucked his walking stick under his arm, giving Genie a pleading grimace that still managed to be charming. "I do hope I am still welcome?"

"Why, of course you are, Mr. Henley, and what magnificent timing too." Genie started to lead Mr. Henley to the dock. "You are just in time for our regatta."

Audrey inspected Lord Cartwright's cousin—and had to admit that he appeared rather affable and handsome. He had a pleasing grin, and his golden hair fell in charming curls over his brow.

"How marvelous!" he exclaimed, much like Lady Kettleridge was wont to do. "I rowed at Oxford. Which of your crews requires another strong back and pair of arms?"

He shed his jacket with enthusiasm, and Basil leaped away from the dock with visible relief. "Please, do take *my* spot, sir."

"Very well," Mr. Henley said, first peering curiously at the valet's eager response. Then, at Audrey and Cassie. "And are these fetching ladies to be our coxswains?"

"Fellow crew mates," Audrey replied. Genie stepped forward to make the introductions, and Audrey noted that Mr. Henley's attention held on her after hearing her name.

"Henley, my good man, you've salvaged the day," Mr. Filmore said. "The duke, Neatham, and Thornton all rode out earlier, depleting our ranks."

"But not to despair; our arms are equally functional," Cassie asserted. Tobias snorted, and she slapped his arm.

"Your Grace, do say you'll join me as coxswain," Lady Veronica said, having joined them. She took Genie by the arm and directed Mr. Henley a bright smile.

Genie touched her temple. "I will have to decline, I'm afraid. I'm feeling rather fatigued. This heat, I'm sure." She did appear pale. Audrey hoped she wasn't unwell. Managing the house party and the upheaval of the last few days had likely taken its toll.

"But, Miss Cynthia," Genie said, calling over to the other young lady. "What say you to directing the second crew as coxswain?"

Her blue eyes grew wide with delight as she popped up from her chair and left her mother's side. "That would be such fun. I accept!"

What had been a candid grin on Cassie's lips now froze and began to melt into a grimace. She turned away toward the lake but not before Audrey noticed her discontent. Did she dislike Cynthia?

Veronica only cleared her throat. She was still latched onto Genie's arm and beaming at Mr. Henley. Belatedly, Genie understood and made the introduction. However, Mr. Henley only gave a polite nod of acknowledgement. He then turned to Mr. Filmore.

"You say the duke and a few guests rode out?"

"There's been a great commotion this week," Westbrook said grumpily. His sour expression had returned in full after last night's incident in the library alcove. He hadn't met Audrey's eyes once all morning, which she did not lament.

"Is that so?" Mr. Henley replied, but Lord Kettleridge waved his arms.

"Let us get on with the race before we all expire from the heat. We shall inform you of the details once we reach the other side."

A tent had been erected on the opposite side of the lake as well as tables and chairs, and a picnic feast. Servants had already rowed out to prepare and greet them after, and a few more boats would ferry over the ladies after the regatta had been run.

Audrey joined Tobias, Lord Kettleridge, and Mr. Henley in one of the crew boats, with Lady Veronica perching on the coxswain's seat. Cassie took a middle position between Lord Westbrook, Mr. Filmore, and Mr. Flint, with Cynthia at the fore. The ladies had all removed their hats, not wanting them to fly away into the lake while rowing.

Squinting against the sun, Audrey gripped her pair of oars in the hooks. She had only rowed once before, with Philip, and that had been a languid outing. Nerves suddenly jangled her, as well as doubt over what Hugh would find at Montague Lodge. Mr. Henley's arrival had as good as stripped him as a possible suspect in Millie's disappearance. He could not have anything to do with the murders and her abduction if he was here, fresh from London. That left Lord Cartwright then. Perhaps he had staged his own kidnapping after all. A sinking disappointment surprised her; she had judged him as sincere in his affections for Millie.

Seated just ahead of her, Mr. Henley looked over his shoulder. "In my experience, rowing with rings of any sort can cause injury or blisters. Best to leave your wedding band or any other piece off with your maid." His eyes drifted pointedly to her hands; she had removed her black lace gloves to keep them from ripping on the oar's handles.

She came alert at the mention of rings. But then pushed aside the prickle of suspicion. As someone experienced with rowing, he was attempting to be helpful.

"Thank you, but my wedding band is quite thin, as you can see," she replied. "I should think I will fare well enough."

Besides, Greer had been far too busy to come down to the lake for the regatta.

Mr. Henley smiled and faced forward, and then, as the butler, Munson, waved a flag while standing at the end of the dock, the teams shoved off. Instantly, the good-natured game changed into pure competition. Veronica seemed to embrace it. Though she cheered on the four crew members as their initial dozen rows propelled them away from shore, she also shouted for them to row faster, harder. "Put your backs into it!" she screamed.

Audrey forced her arms and shoulders to row just as rapidly as the others in her boat, to keep pace and not throw off the cadence of the crew's flight across the surface. Water splashed and whipped from the oars with every upward slice, sprinkling her face. She welcomed the cooling dashes especially as she broke into a sweat. Her heart drummed rapidly as she rowed, her palms, gripping the quickly dampening wooden oars, creating an uncomfortable friction.

Perhaps this had not been the best idea after all. And Mr. Henley had been quite right—the continuous rubbing of her skin around her wedding band *was* growing unpleasant.

Nearly parallel to them, though just a little further ahead, the other crew skimmed through the water. Cynthia echoed Veronica's cheers and instruction, and as Audrey took a few quick glimpses, she saw Cassie doing quite well, her dark blond hair coming loose from her pins and combs. She let out a whoop of laughter, and it fed Audrey's soul to hear it; she had been melancholy for so long. With a burst of excitement, Audrey regained her flagging strength and cut her oars into the water with renewed vigor.

The opposite shore was fast approaching. Her muscles seared red hot, and she longed to simply plunge bodily into the water to cool off. At the shoreline, Sir's shorter form was among the others shouting and clapping, and Audrey once more dug into a well of reserved strength to make the final push with the crew. Their boat passed the end of the dock a mere second before Cassie's boat, and a great cheer went up among the gathered servants. With more relief and elation than she had ever felt, Audrey dropped her oars in their brackets and, despite her aching body, could not stop smiling and laughing.

"Well done!" Mr. Henley shouted.

"Huzzah! Huzzah!" Tobias chanted.

Lord Westbrook was the only one in the other boat not smiling. The others patted each other, and Cassie too, on the back.

"They won by a hair," Cassie said as she was helped from her boat. Mr. Henley, already on the dock, stooped to hand Audrey up.

"A hair was all we needed," he commented with a goading grin toward Cassie. "You ladies are deceivingly robust. Well done."

Audrey wasn't certain she liked being called robust, but

it was clearly meant as a compliment and she thanked him. However, he held onto her hand a moment longer than necessary, his attention again drifting toward her fingers. Discomfited, Audrey retracted her hand and brushed her skirt—and it was only then that she realized it was utterly soaked. The water splashing off the oars had drenched it.

"Here you are, duchess." Sir edged past Mr. Henley and extended a length of toweling.

"Excellent foresight, Sir. Thank you."

"I am ready for a rematch," Cassie said, the color high in her cheeks. Audrey laughed.

"My dear Cassie, you're just as competitive as Michael."

"And where has the duke and the others gone off to?" Mr. Henley asked, his forehead beading with sweat, his shirt-sleeves dampened by the same, as well as by lake water.

Lord Kettleridge also accepted a towel from a footman, and while drying the back of his neck answered, "Pyke-on-Wending. Montague Lodge, in fact."

Had Mr. Henley not been reaching for the towel being extended to him, Audrey might have missed his reaction. He went still, his arm freezing mid-grasp—before then tugging the towel from the footman's hand.

"Whatever for?" he asked, but just as Kettleridge began to inform Mr. Henley of the events of the last handful of days, a gentle hand rested on Audrey's shoulder.

Cassie had taken two glasses of ratafia from a footman, one of which she extended to Audrey. "Cheers," she said as Audrey accepted her small glass. Mr. Henley and Kettleridge had been joined by Mr. Filmore and they were ambling toward the grassy banking and a refreshments table. Though she wanted to follow and observe Mr. Henley as he heard about Millie's abduction, Cassie's next words stole her attention thoroughly.

"I want to explain about Mr. Knowlton." Her voice was strained and soft. Her energy and delight from the regatta had transformed into something more dismal.

He was *Mr. Knowlton* now, when before, she had referred to him as William.

"It is over between the two of you?" Audrey guessed.

She flattened her lips and nodded. "He isn't a cad, as Toby called him," she said, leading Audrey onto the grass and into the shade of an awning. The other ladies, soon to join them, were currently being rowed in smaller boats across the lake, George and his nursemaid among them.

Audrey kept her voice low. "What happened?"

"It's inconsequential, really." Cassie sipped her drink and attempted an insouciant shrug, but it came across as forced. She *did* care. Whatever happened, it wasn't minor to her.

"You two were smitten," Audrey reminded her. "Or so it appeared."

In fact, an official proposal had been expected early in the summer. It had not come to pass, but Audrey had assumed it was the result of William and Cassie simply being young. He was but twenty-two and Cassie, not yet twenty.

"I believe he was smitten," she said after a moment. "And I wish I could say the same. More than anything I wish I could say it."

"But you weren't. Not like he was?"

She shook her head, and Audrey could now see the truth: Cassie felt guilty for not matching William in his affections for her.

"These things cannot be forced," she said to her. "You were being honest with him. It was a kindness, in the end."

"I know. William is wonderful, handsome, kind. I should have been in love. And now, with his attentions having turned elsewhere, I wonder if I've bungled everything." Her eyes drifted toward Lady Veronica and Cynthia, who were waiting on the dock for other ladies. Understanding tolled through Audrey.

"Miss Stewart?"

Cassie nodded. "They became acquainted while I was in Brighton." She sighed. "But Audrey, I just...I'm not sure I can ever trust any man again. Not after..."

Audrey lowered herself into one of the chairs that had been set out and, taking Cassie's arm, invited her to sit next to her. "Not all men are like Renfry."

The wretched man had used Cassie horribly, making vows of love and marriage to entice her into his bed. To gain her trust. With a twinge of apprehension, Audrey compared her own night with Hugh to what must have happened with Cassie and Lord Renfry. She could now understand how easily a woman could be led. Renfry and Hugh were utter opposites, however. Hugh's intentions were honorable. Honest. Should she, as Cassie did, ever discover otherwise... With that unsettling thought, Audrey's compassion for her young sister-in-law deepened.

"I know," Cassie said. "Logically, I know."

And yet, the wounds he'd caused had not yet healed.

"But for now," she went on, a glimmer of her energy returning. "I plan to reach my majority in less than two years and access my dowry."

"And what will you do with it?" Audrey asked, truly curious. A woman making her own way in the world would be no easy feat. And if Michael did not approve of her plan, he could make it difficult for her to take control of her own fortune.

Cassie shrugged, this time believably. "I don't know just yet. Perhaps I will travel the Continent. Become an artist."

"You hate painting."

Cassie laughed. "I do, don't I? Well then, I'll try sculpture."

Now this sounded more like the Cassie that Audrey knew. Light and bubbly, full of life. Perhaps William Knowlton had not been the one to capture Cassie's heart, but Audrey hoped that she would not close herself off to the possibility for love.

"You will think of something, and whatever it is, I hope it fulfills you," she said, bringing her glass of ratafia to her lips. At the same time, she looked to the dock, where Lady Kettleridge, Mrs. Stewart, Mrs. Filmore, and Genie all gathered. A footman rowing George and his nursemaid had nearly reached the dock too.

Audrey lowered her glass. One of the boats the ladies had taken was now several yards into a return crossing to the opposite shore, and at the oars was Mr. Henley. Veronica sat opposite him, her mother's parasol shielding her from the sun.

"Poor girl is feeling a bit faint from the race," Lady Kettleridge exclaimed, her voice carrying as she and Mrs. Filmore ambled toward the awning.

Cassie snorted softly. "I can't understand why. She only worked her jaw."

Audrey kept her eyes on Mr. Henley's back. He would

have heard all there was to tell about the murders and Millie's disappearance by now. Perhaps he was simply escorting a wilting young lady back to the main house. But Audrey's instinct argued against it. She stood, setting down her glass. "Cassie, I think I'll return to the house as well, to change out of this damp gown. Would you like to join me?"

"Gracious, yes. Before the squawking ladies descend. Hurry."

Audrey and Cassie made their way to the dock, Sir falling in beside them, ready to assist. No doubt at Hugh's instruction.

"Sir, how are your arms feeling?"

The boy frowned. "My arms?"

"I'm sorry to say mine have turned to aspic. Can you take us across the lake?"

"Sure thing, duchess. So long as I don't dump myself in. Can't swim." His attention jumped to the boat bearing Mr. Henley and Veronica to shore. Mindful of Cassie's presence, the boy said nothing, but he met Audrey's eyes and arched a brow, jutting his chin toward the boat halfway across the lake. Audrey nodded, grateful for his intellect and candor.

Whatever Mr. Henley was up to, she didn't want to let him out of her sight.

SIXTEEN

There was something curiously lacking at Pyke-on-Wending. Though twice the size of Moorsly, as Hugh rode through the main roads, he noted the quiet of the streets and surrounding cottages. With signs naming taverns, a blacksmith and wheelwright, a haberdasher and grocer, and several other shops, he would have expected more people out and about, more activity and enterprise. He held his tongue, observing the sleepy surroundings as he, Thornton, and Fournier carried on north of the village, to where a large sawmill perched on the River Wending. Here as well there was little sign of industry.

"Montague is landowner here?" Hugh asked as Fournier peered at the mill. The moss-covered water wheel looked as if it had been still for some time.

"Yes. I had not realized the extent of its decline."

"What have you heard?" Thornton asked.

Like Hugh and Fournier, he'd discarded his coat in the oppressive heat and folded it into his saddle bag. His medical satchel had been stored there as well, brought out of precaution.

"It's been rumored the marquess's parsimonious manner had started to have an impact," the duke replied, gesturing to the mill as they passed it. "This place was once bustling, every cottage filled with workers, for the mill, the manor house, the shops."

Landowners were charged with keeping up the villages that built up on their estates; that meant investing in repairs, in new industry, and in the laborers and families making it their home. If neglected, the villagers would move on and the village itself would decay.

"Either Montague doesn't care to keep the place up, or he doesn't have the funds to do so," Hugh said, his mind turning again to the investment venture of Henley's. Was it a way to bolster the family coffers? And why should Henley care, as he was not heir?

"Well we certainly can't ask him, as the marquess is not in residence," Fournier said. His attitude on their outing had been consistent: he thought it a waste of time.

The duke had not been eager to join them. So much so that he had suggested riding out after the regatta. But Hugh, despising the feeling of inertia, had argued against it, and Fournier had relented, though not without grumbling. For all of his differences from Philip, Michael was similarly unsmiling and stern.

Hugh still couldn't quite grasp the enormous certitude Philip must have possessed to do what he had. To abandon his entire life in favor of something unknown and precarious took conviction. Anger still seethed within him when he thought of how selfish the duke had been to leave Audrey to continue with the farce and keep his secret, all on her own. At the same time, if Philip had not made that decision, Hugh and Audrey would still be where they'd been before. Unable to love anyone else, and yet unable to love each other. Another state of inertia he had grown frustrated with.

When they encountered a high stone wall running along the lane, Hugh figured they were close to the entrance to Montague Lodge. Vines ran over the top, unkempt. At a gap in the border wall, they turned, and found the greenery and tree limbs equally unmaintained along the drive. It was a notable difference to Greenbriar and Fournier Downs, where each blade of grass was clipped to perfection, every errant weed plucked, and every fading bloom removed. At Cranleigh, the Neatham country estate, the gardeners kept the lawns and gardens swept, though they were a bit wilder. Purposefully so. Montague Lodge, when the main house appeared, simply gave the impression of neglect. Much like Pyke-on-Wending.

They reached the main house, which did not appear much like a lodge at all. At least not the hunting lodge Hugh's father had frequented on Cranleigh's property. That structure was little more than wattle and daub with dark wooden timbers that blended into the surrounding woodland. This lodge was a three-story brick square with clean lines and large windows. It was styled more like a manor house.

No servants appeared to greet them as they dismounted, and it took a minute or more for someone to open the door after Hugh brought down the brass knocker. The man, dressed in the black livery of a butler, bowed in greeting after Fournier presented his card, and they were shown into the entrance foyer. When the duke then asked if his lordship was at home, the butler announced what Fournier had been saying all along: "My lord is not in residence this summer, Your Grace."

"Any sightings of people on the land the last week or so? Strangers? Any odd noises?" Hugh asked.

The butler frowned. "No, my lord—as I have told the other men who came asking the same questions a few days ago."

Fournier sent Hugh a look that was the epitome of *"See? I told you."* Hugh brushed it aside.

"What about Mr. Robert Henley?" he asked next.

The butler's annoyed expression changed over to one of thought. "He departed five days ago, my lord."

Hugh had not expected that answer. It momentarily silenced him as his mind absorbed the information.

"What was his destination?" Thornton asked.

"London, I was told. Then on to Dover."

"He is leaving the country?" Hugh asked, surprised yet again. Dover was one of England's primary ports.

"We have reduced the staff, taking into consideration Lord Montague's absence, but we had expected Mr. Henley to stay for a short spell. As it was, he was here but for a fortnight." The butler's tone betrayed a hint of displeasure.

So, Henley had been here for at least two weeks before leaving. Hugh looked to Fournier, whose face pinched with contemplation. "He sent Genie his regrets within that time," the duke supplied.

"Did he say why?" Hugh asked, but Fournier shook his head.

Something had changed his mind about the house party,

and he was not only fleeing to London, but out of the country.

"Is there anything more I can do for you, Your Grace? My lords? Tea, perhaps?" the butler inquired.

"No, thank you for your time. We will see ourselves out," Fournier said. But though the others turned to leave, Hugh's feet stayed planted to the parquet flooring.

"His valet," he said, then realizing he'd only mumbled, said louder, "Mr. Henley's valet. Did he leave for London with his lordship?"

The butler blinked and appeared lost for words for a moment. But then recovered. "I am afraid not."

"He is here then?"

"No, I apologize, my lord, his valet recently left his position."

Hugh still did not move. He felt as though each revelation was adding weight to his legs, holding him in place. The valet left?

"How recently?"

"In July, my lord."

A possibility breathed to life in his mind. "Do you know where he went?"

The man shook his head. "He gave no indication."

"The valet's name. Was it Samuel? Lord Cartwright's former valet?"

A light flickered in the butler's eyes. "Indeed. Is there any trouble with him, my lord?"

Samuel. Presumably called *Sammy,* Hugh imagined. The mixed-up pieces of the investigation began to lock together at last. Hugh finally came unstuck from the floor. "Thank you, you've been very helpful."

He started toward the door, where Fournier and Thornton waited for him. Thornton, however, had seemed to think of something more.

"One more question," he said. "This is not the lodge for which the estate is named, is it?"

"Oh, no, my lord. The lodge itself is in the parkland, off the wooded lane. Sadly, it has fallen into disuse. With his lordship's ague and poor lungs, the comforts of the manor house have appealed to him more over the last decade."

Thornton grinned and set his hat back upon his head. "Thank you. As my friend said, you've been most helpful."

The door had closed behind them, and Hugh had mounted his horse before eyeing Thornton. "Well done."

"And who is Samuel?" Thornton asked, tipping the brim of his hat in acknowledgment of the compliment.

"I suspect he is Lady Redding's dead driver."

"My god," Fournier muttered.

"They called him Sammy at Reddingate," Hugh explained as they turned their mounts toward the drive. But they were not leaving. "He was new on staff."

"Why in hell would Henley's valet leave to become a driver at Reddingate?" Fournier asked.

"I think he was placed there," Hugh replied as they trotted along the drive. The close-set trees and boughs made it appear tunnel-like and shaded them from the glaring sun.

"Placed? By whom and for what purpose?" the duke asked.

"Cartwright said three people knew Lady Redding had kept the purple diamond: himself, the lady, and his valet."

"After Cartwright left for India, his valet might have been reassigned. To his cousin?" Thornton said.

"Montague has always preferred Henley, according to Cartwright. It makes sense that once his heir was out of the picture, he would shift his only other grandson into the role."

"But Henley cannot inherit, preferred or not," Fournier reminded them. "Unless something untoward befell Cartwright."

"What would either of them inherit?" Hugh said. "Did you hear the butler mentioning Montague's ailments? Reduced staff? They sounded like excuses to me. I'm willing to wager Montague's fortune has been depleting over the last decade, and Henley is aware of it."

"Montague's two children are both dead," Fournier said. "His heir is Cartwright, and the next in line is Henley, who would ostensibly be given an annuity from Montague."

"But if those coffers were rapidly diminishing, Henley's involvement in the silver mine speculation would make sense," Thornton said. "Going to these lengths to steal a ring worth at best a few thousand pounds makes no sense."

"Exactly. Why send his valet to Reddingate to spy on Lady Redding?" Fournier scoffed. "I cannot believe it. To what end?"

They were correct. Hugh shook his head. "I don't know. It has to do with the diamond, but one jewel could not repair a failing town or fill the marquess's coffers again. It would not give Henley lasting security."

Fournier pulled up short at a small bridge they had crossed earlier on the way toward the manor. The river beneath flowed swiftly over mossy rocks. "There," he said, jutting his chin toward an opening within the trees, just before the bridge. "The butler said the lodge was down the wooded lane. That looks to be a turn off."

Directing his horse closer, Hugh saw a narrow lane overrun with grass and vines. Dual furrows cut into the ground from cart wheels of ages past were visible, along with fresher tracks. Hugh listened to the burbling river another moment.

"That is the Wending?" he asked. Fournier nodded. "It runs down to Moorsly." Another nod. And then Fournier frowned as he comprehended.

"The maid. She was pulled from the river."

In silent agreement, they turned their mounts down the wooded lane. As they followed the ruts, Hugh noted indentations from shoed horses. This lane had been recently accessed. After several minutes, all spent in complete silence, a structure came into view through the trees. Built of stone and timber, the lodge did appear to be in disuse. If it weren't for the swishing tail of a horse, sticking out from behind unkempt hedges near the stables, Hugh might have thought his hunch was off. But as they turned into the trees off the lane and dismounted, his skin prickled. This was where Millie was being kept. He could feel it.

"Thornton," Hugh whispered. "Ready your pistol."

His friend drew the weapon from his hip holster as Hugh did the same. Fournier started to draw his, though Hugh held up a hand to stay him.

"Your Grace, perhaps you should stay with the horses."

"May I remind you, I was a lieutenant in His Majesty's army," he replied tightly. "I am coming with you."

"Very well. But tuck away your weapon. Appearing

unarmed may help our approach," Hugh said, coming up with a plan.

A few minutes later, the Duke of Fournier walked into the clearing, approaching the lodge directly while calling out, "Hello? Is anyone in?"

Hugh moved through the trees, to the left of the lodge. Thornton was hidden within the green foliage to the right, on a path toward the stables.

The duke had removed his hat and jacket, mussed his hair, and rolled up his shirtsleeves to give the appearance of a thoroughly befuddled traveler. "I say, is anyone in? I'm afraid my horse has thrown a shoe and injured its leg. I'm looking for assistance."

His voice carried in the quiet clearing. For several moments more, Hugh's heart pounded. But then, the front door opened. A man emerged. He wore a threadbare hat, workaday clothes, and an unkempt beard. He did not look to be a servant, but a disheveled footpad. Fournier, however, reacted just as planned.

"Oh, jolly good! Hallo, there. I do apologize for the intrusion—"

"Nobody's here what can help you," the man said, his voice gruff and bothered. Hugh crossed from the trees and pressed close to the side of the lodge, out of the man's line of sight.

"That is a pity," Fournier said. "A true pity. My horse is quite lame. Are you sure you could not round someone up?"

"I said, ain't nobody here. You've got to go back the way you've come and find someplace else."

Hugh came around the corner, his pistol drawn and aimed at the man's back. "Do not move." As expected, the man didn't obey. He spun around, his hand reaching under his coat.

"I wouldn't," Thornton said as he emerged from the opposite corner of the lodge. The man stilled.

"How many more are inside?" Hugh asked.

The man grimaced. "Just me."

"On your belly," Hugh commanded, not believing him for an instant. The man obeyed this time, and with the portions of rein he'd cut free a few minutes before, Fournier hurried forward to bind the man's hands and ankles.

"The truth this time," Hugh said. "Who else is posted guard here?"

With his cheek to the gravel, the man gritted out, "Told you. Just me. Me and the lord in there."

The lord. *Cartwright?* Hugh met Thornton's skeptical look and nodded toward the back of the lodge. Thornton moved off, to go around and inspect for others. Hugh and Fournier left the man bound on the gravel and entered through the front door. The place was dark and musty, the stone walls covered with trophies of hunts past. Elk and deer stared down at them with glassy eyes from their mounted backings and a hare was perched mid-leap on a nearby table. A bear stood on its hind legs in the corner, its paws raised into the air, claws extended.

Most of the furniture had been covered with sheets, aligning with the butler's claim that the place had fallen into disuse. But scuffing noises came from an adjacent room. Hugh held his pistol at the ready and followed the sounds.

When he entered the room—a great hall with a massive hearth at one end—he lowered his flintlock. "Cartwright."

The man sat in a cane-backed chair, arms tied behind

him and ankles bound to the chair's front legs. A strip of fabric had been wrapped around his mouth and knotted behind his head. He began to thrash and rattle the chair, his grunts and muffled words incoherent.

Hugh crossed the room and ripped the gag from his mouth. He heaved a gulp of air and began speaking at once.

"It's Robert. My cousin," he said, his voice rough and raspy. A mottled bruise colored his eye, and his nose appeared broken with crusted blood over the bridge. His lower lip had also been split. He hadn't turned over his own room at the Hare and Crown after all.

"Henley?"

Cartwright nodded wildly. "He's lost his mind. The silver mine. It's a scam. He's been swindled. He has Millie," he said, his sentences short and urgent. "Untie me, we have to go after them!"

Fournier swore under his breath as he joined them. "The silver mine? My god, several men have sunk small fortunes into that venture."

"And he's lost it all," Hugh said, circling the chair to untie Cartwright's wrists. As soon as he was free, Cartwright leaned forward and began loosening the knots at his ankles.

"That is why he's fleeing England," Fournier said.

Thornton entered the great hall then. "There is no one else here."

"When did Henley leave?" Hugh asked, his pulse again increasing as a prediction formed. "And why did he take Lady Redding?"

"This morning." Cartwright threw off the binding ropes and stood, though he winced and braced his ribs. He'd been beaten badly.

"He took her as leveraging of a sort. She didn't want to tell him where the ring was, but when he threatened to kill me, she..." Cartwright closed his eyes and rubbed his bloody temple. He'd been dragged here and used, no doubt, to convince Millie to give up the location of the ring. "She didn't have a choice."

The hours it had taken to ride to Montague Lodge...they had passed several coaches on the way.

Hugh's blood went to ice. "He's gone to Greenbriar."

Cartwright nodded. "The ring is there. Millie's sister, Audrey...she has had it all along."

CHAPTER

SEVENTEEN

L aughter and chatter carried across the small lake. The inarticulate distance of it had an isolating effect on Audrey as she and Cassie started up the slope of the lawn toward the main house. Sir was behind them, having stopped to tie up the boat next to its match, emptied several minutes before when Veronica and Mr. Henley reached shore.

Audrey had watched from her seat in the boat as Mr. Henley handed Veronica from the small vessel. They had quickly disappeared back up to the main house as Sir had finished crossing the lake. A few times, Cassie inquired if he would like assistance. He'd started off politely declining, but by the fourth time, his answer had transformed into a full-on scowl.

"He is a little rapscallion, isn't he?" Cassie said now, looking over her shoulder at Sir.

Audrey murmured her agreement, though her mind was still hinged on Mr. Henley and his odd appearance at Greenbriar. It was strange, wasn't it, that he had arrived at the shore without a footman leading him down? Or perhaps because Munson was already at the lake, along with several more footmen, it hadn't been seen as necessary.

"The viscount seems to have a soft spot for him," Cassie observed. "You don't think he's...you know...*his*?"

Shock ruptured Audrey's direction of thought, and she gaped at Cassie. "Hugh's *son*? No! Heavens, no."

Cassie grinned widely. "Well, it wouldn't be so shocking, would it? The late viscount did take on his illegitimate child as a ward."

"Hugh isn't illegitimate," Audrey reminded her.

"Yes, we know that *now*," she said. Then she nudged Audrey's arm. "There is something between the two of you. Isn't there?"

Cassie pressed her lips in a crafty little grin when Audrey again gaped at her.

"Oh, don't try to deny it," she went on. "And don't think for a moment I would be displeased. I know you loved my brother. He would want you to be happy—"

Audrey pulled her arm from Cassie's, flustered, her tongue utterly tied in knots.

Cassie's grin faded. "I'm sorry. I shouldn't have said that. It was heartless of me."

"No, I'm not upset. Truly. I just..." *Feel inconceivably guilty for pretending your brother is dead.* "I need to change out of these wet clothes. Forgive me, I'll see you back down at the lake shortly. We'll row back over together?"

She dashed off before Cassie could reply. The cool air of the house chilled her as she took the stairs to the landing, her mind awhirl with how rude and inane she must have sounded. Why should she be shocked if others could see that there was something between her and Hugh? It was why Lady Veronica had all but declared war on her, after all.

Audrey decided she would change her gown, as she'd told Cassie she would, and then search for Mr. Henley. But as she turned at the newel post and started along the empty landing toward her room, something moved in her side vision. She responded too slowly—and a hand wrapped firmly around her left arm. Mr. Henley practically adhered himself to her side in an instant, and something hard poked into her hip.

"This is regrettable, Your Grace, but I've run out of time."

"Mr. Henley, what are you—"

"Hush." He forced them to a stop. "If you cooperate, I will leave you unharmed."

Panic flared, sending her pulse streaming. She should have trusted her earlier instinct.

"You have Millie," she said.

He ignored her. "All I require is the ring. The one your sister gave you."

"I have no such ring." Her eyes swept the landing. Her room was straight ahead. Greer was likely inside, her duties having kept her from the regatta.

Mr. Henley's grip on her arm bruised. "Do not play games. I know you have it."

"I am being truthful. Why would my sister give me a ring?"

"She did so without your knowledge. She hid it in something you treasure. Something you take with you everywhere and would never be rid of."

Her mind galloped as she tried to determine what item he could mean.

"A shell," Mr. Henley hissed in her ear. "She said it is in your shell."

The small hairs along Audrey's arms stood on end and a low whirring noise filled her ears. *Her shell*. The nautilus shell James had given her?

"Ah yes, you understand now, don't you?" Mr. Henley said. "Good. Now, let us go get it."

He urged them forward again, but Audrey dug in her heels. With Greer possibly waiting in the bedchamber, she would not bring this man close. She would not risk her maid's life. Not even when the barrel of the flintlock pistol pushed harder into her waist.

"It isn't here. Not at Greenbriar."

"Then *where*?" he demanded.

Her mind went blank. And then, her mouth formed an answer: "Fournier Downs."

It was a lie. The shell *was* here, just inside her bedchamber, in the writing box she took with her everywhere. Just as Millie had told Mr. Henley. The ring was hidden *inside* the shell? Audrey couldn't comprehend it. And for the moment, the discovery did not matter. She only had to get this man as far from Greenbriar and the people here as possible. Good heavens...Cassie could be on her way to her own bedchamber. She might be ascending the stairs any moment.

"Then we will go to Hertfordshire," Mr. Henley said, and turned roughly, back toward the main stairs. "Do as I say. Cause a scene, and your sister will meet the same end as her maid. Is that understood?"

Audrey nodded, her head jerking tightly as a sickening concoction of terror and relief flooded her. Millie was alive, but he had killed Celine. The driver, too. For the ring?

The stairs were blessedly empty. Cassie must have gone in another direction to her room, or perhaps not to her room at all. They approached the front door and a footman stationed there. Mr. Henley had already hooked Audrey's arm, and though the hard point of the pistol disappeared from her hip, she knew the weapon was still a danger. She tempered the inclination to struggle and shout for the footman's help. But Mr. Henley had a pistol, and he'd already killed two people—servants, at that. So, Audrey smiled thinly as the footman bowed and opened the door for them to pass through.

"A turn around the gardens sounds like a lovely idea," Mr. Henley said with false politeness as they passed. And then, the door was shutting behind them.

"Where is my sister?" Audrey asked as they walked not toward the gardens, but the long drive. There was no one about, and with most of the servants at the lake, they would likely go unobserved as they walked away.

"You will see her shortly," was all he replied as he increased their pace. He was taking no chances, and the returned poke of the pistol proved it.

Despite everything, relief that she would see Millie momentarily buoyed her. If, of course, he was telling the truth. Considering how readily and easily *she* had lied regarding the nautilus shell's location, she would take his words with a grain of salt. It was possible he, too, was simply telling her what she wished to hear in order to get her to cooperate.

"Where are we walking?" she asked as their pace grew increasingly harried. They were now out of view of the main house, surrounded by woods on one side and lawns on the other. The knolls of the grounds obscured a view of the lake and the other guests there.

Mr. Henley did not reply, and Audrey, breathless as she was from the rapid pace and the edge of panic, didn't repeat her question. He had arrived at Greenbriar *on foot*? He had also likely not applied at the front door, but simply walked down to the lake. His missing conveyance would have been of concern to the footman posted at the entrance door.

Finally, as sweat began to trickle down her back and gather on her brow, he directed them off the main drive and into a stand of trees. The trunks of the mixed whitebeams and firs were widely spaced—wide enough for a coach and a pair of horses to wait, obscured. A man sat ready in the driver's box; he acknowledged them with a nod as Mr. Henley shoved Audrey toward the coach. When he opened the door and jostled her up inside, she tripped on the hem of her skirt. She landed on her knee but caught herself from falling flat by grasping the bench cushion. When everything stilled, she was met with her sister's fearful eyes and tear-streaked face.

"Millie?" She heaved herself up off the floor and onto the bench. Her sister cried out, but a gag muffled her. Rope bound her ankles and wrists. Her auburn hair was a loose mess, her cheeks and eyes red and puffy, her gown wrinkled and dusty.

"Go," Mr. Henley barked to his driver as soon as he'd dropped onto the bench across from them. The driver cracked the reins, and the coach jolted forward to clear the tree cover.

Audrey removed the gag from Millie's mouth and her sister's sobs unleashed.

"Oh, sister!" she gasped. "I am so very sorry. I didn't want to tell him. I would never have, but they had Reggie and—"

"Enough with your blubbering," Mr. Henley said harshly. He had his pistol out fully now, the weapon aimed at them. He glared at Audrey, all affability gone. "She remains bound."

"Don't you think that will look suspicious if we meet anyone on the road?" Audrey replied. "The magistrate, Sir Ridley, perhaps? He is due back to Greenbriar today," she lied through her teeth. "Should he wish to speak to us, and my sister is trussed up like a sow—"

"Very well, untie her. Just shut up."

The charm he had showered upon the regatta party had vanished. Callous impatience now transformed his previously handsome visage into something ugly.

Audrey worked at the knots binding Millie's wrists, then bent to untie her ankles. The ropes had left raw marks on her skin and frayed her stockings, evidence that she had been tied up for much of the past few days.

As the driver took them down Greenbriar's lane at a frantic clip, rocking them wildly, Audrey turned her attention to what would happen once Mr. Henley realized he had been tricked. It would be hours to Fournier Downs. Half the day, at least. She had succeeded at drawing him away from Greenbriar, but she and Millie were still in danger.

"All this for a ring?" she asked, her heart in her throat as she broke Mr. Henley's order to shut up.

He only glowered. "Do you have any notion how much that diamond is worth?"

If he required money so desperately, there could be only one reason why. "The silver venture. It isn't going well, is it?"

"I told you to be quiet," he seethed.

She bit her tongue as it all came together. Mr. Henley had sunk his fortune into the speculation. So had many other peers. "The mine has failed?"

His eyes shone as he adjusted the pistol. But before he could instruct her to keep quiet again, Millie spoke.

"There is no mine," she said, her voice raspy from disuse. "There never was. I've heard him talking. He was conned into investing, and then, thinking it all aboveboard, got others to invest too. Accepted their money and gave it to the swindler."

"Shut up," he barked.

"Why? You are only going to kill us anyway. Just as you killed Celine and Sammy."

Audrey gripped her sister's arm. "And Lord Cartwright?"

Tears welled in Millie's eyes. "He is alive. But only because I told them about James's shell. I didn't want to. I tried to keep you out of it."

Audrey understood now. Knowing that Lord Cartwright had gone to Haverfield with the intent to meet with Millie, Mr. Henley and his accomplices had tracked him to the area and abducted him. They had then threatened to kill him if Millie did not confess. Faced with that choice, Millie's resolve had crumbled. Audrey could not honestly say hers would not have, especially if Mr. Henley had held Hugh at the end of his pistol.

Hugh. He was nowhere near Greenbriar. If she was going to get herself and Millie out of this situation alive, she had no choice but to do it on her own. The tension stringing Mr. Henley into tight knots may be able to aid her.

"You plan to pawn the ring and flee England," Audrey

said, "rather than face the men you've inadvertently swindled and admit yourself equally deceived?"

He scoffed. "I partnered with Teague, and now, he is gone. Vanished with all our money. Who do you think would be prosecuted for the scheme once it is made known?"

Had Mr. Henley simply been duped and defrauded, Audrey might have felt pity for him. But his actions to cover up his own wrongdoing, his own folly, had ruined any chance of that.

"Why shoot the driver? Why not just make it look like a regular highway robbery and leave him unharmed?" she asked.

"My men had their orders for good reason. Samuel made the mistake of starting to care for Miss Woods. Started to feel a sense of guilt at the deception," he said, still pouting. "I could not risk that he would speak of it in the future."

Samuel. Not *Sammy*, as Millie had called him. A new hire, Millie's butler had said when Audrey and Hugh had been at Reddingate. Mr. Henley had known him. Samuel had been working *for him*.

Her lips parted in understanding. "Sammy was Lord Cartwright's former valet. Now *your* valet."

Millie balked. "Reggie's *valet* became my driver?"

"You didn't recognize him?" Audrey asked. Her sister looked offended.

"I had never met Reggie's valet. I had no idea!"

"But he knew you had kept the ring. And he told you, Mr. Henley, didn't he? You sent him to Reddingate to steal it."

"The cad charmed my maid and convinced her to search my room," Millie said, her jaw tight. "She found Reggie's letter asking about the ring, and my response that it was at Greenbriar. That I needed to fetch it before meeting him at Haverfield."

Audrey exhaled. So that was how Celine had betrayed Millie. She'd told Samuel, who in turn informed Mr. Henley, who then sent his accomplices to waylay Millie's coach.

"I suppose Celine knew too much as well," Audrey said, disgusted by the memory of the maid's body lain out in that Moorsly barn, and the vision the silver pendant had shown her. She and Samuel had not been worth more than the information they'd provided. It was a bald display of Mr. Henley's obscene lack of mercy.

"All this time, grandfather believed Reggie took it with him when he blew off to India and cut us out of his life."

"Lord Montague had tried to steal it from Lord Cartwright once," Audrey said. "He wasn't going to allow his grandfather the chance again."

Mr. Henley sneered. "The ring was the least Reggie could give Grandfather for taking him in, for enduring the shame of his heir's tainted progeny."

Audrey recoiled from his hateful outburst while Millie leaned forward, livid.

"The only shameful thing is your shallow heart," Millie said. "He is your family. Your blood—"

"Sit back and seal your lips, viscountess," Mr. Henley hissed.

Millie snapped back in her seat, her anger palpable.

But the mention of Lord Montague led Audrey to another quandary. "Surely, you could have repaid the others' lost investments if you'd asked the marquess's for assistance? Why take such drastic measures?"

Mr. Henley snorted derisive laughter. "Grandfather? He is destitute! He's sold everything that is not entailed, right down to the furniture. Hell, if his properties weren't entailed, he'd have sold them too."

"I see. And yet your plans don't include helping your grandfather, only yourself."

"Spare me your moral superiority," he said. "He willingly buried himself, without a second thought for me. That ring will fetch a tidy sum, enough to purchase a new life abroad. It is all I have left to me."

"You are despicable." Millie fairly trembled with impotent rage.

Mr. Henley shifted his jaw, and for a terrifying moment, Audrey thought he might pull the trigger. But he only sighed. "You know, none of this would have been so difficult if Lady Redding only told my men where the ring was straightaway. Instead, Your Grace, your devoted sister refused to speak. Refused to give you up as keeper of the diamond, unwitting as you were."

Millie tucked her chin and closed her eyes, her face contorting again with a suppressed sob. Audrey covered her sister's hand. She felt no anger toward her for their circumstances. When Millie opened her eyes, a smile wobbled over her lips.

"You carried that shell with you everywhere. Treated it like a good luck charm."

She had, even more so after James was gone. It surprised her that Millie had noticed. She'd always believed she was invisible to her older sister.

"I couldn't take the chance of one of my maids noticing the ring, especially after that scandal with Reggie's arrest," she went on. "And you know how Mother is always changing the décor at Haverfield. I could not keep it there and risk it being thrown away or removed from the house."

Her sister's chin trembled. This was a side of Millie she had never seen. Emotional. Vulnerable. Her sister had always been so severe, so rigid. That she would have tried to protect Audrey from Mr. Henley and his thugs, at her own expense, made her wonder what other hidden depths she possessed.

If she wanted to find out, she needed to keep them both alive. That meant not playing into Mr. Henley's hands.

She set her jaw and said, "I knew."

Millie's eyes widened. "You knew?"

"I did. All along, I knew. I found the ring several years ago."

Mr. Henley hinged forward. "*What?*"

Recklessly—something Hugh had accused her of being countless times—Audrey plunged forward with her ruse, even though to what end was not yet clear.

"The ring must have shifted within the shell. I heard it rattling inside, and I pulled it free. I had no idea it belonged to you," Audrey said, the words rushing out just as quickly as she was cobbling together a plan.

"Where is it?" A new, dangerous edge dragged his voice low.

She held her breath. Then took the plunge. "I don't know. I sold it."

Silence. Their captor froze. Then, he erupted with a howl so grating and pained that Audrey winced and clapped her hands over her ears. Millie yelped and cowered as Mr. Henley's face turned a mottled red, a vein standing out on his forehead.

"You are lying," he shouted, the pistol practically shaking as he aimed it at her head.

"I wish I was. But I did sell it. For a vast sum, too. I hid the money from everyone, even my husband."

"Why would you do that?" he asked, his suspicion still surging.

"My husband would already gain my dowry. Why give him this, too?" she replied with a single shoulder shrug. "I wasn't sure at the time how he managed his finances. If he might gamble it all away."

Mr. Henley shook his head, still not convinced. She had to admit, it was a flimsy excuse. "You said it was at Fournier Downs," he reminded her.

"The money it fetched is there."

He gnashed his teeth against a furious reply, and instead asked, "How much is left?"

The flush from his cheeks drained as he no doubt worried his escape plot had been sunk. And if it had, he would not need to keep either hostage alive. Audrey had to salvage things, and quickly.

"Just over five thousand," she answered, thinking of the initial investment sum for the silver mine. She prayed it would be significant enough to stay him. The long exhalation he emitted hinted that it was.

"I won't look a gift horse in the mouth," he grated out, sitting back against the squabs. "The ring already changed over into pounds sterling will hasten my departure."

"Good. Now then, have your driver pull over."

Mr. Henley peered at her as though she'd spoken an unknown language. "Come again?"

"Pull over. If you want me to lead you to the money, you will let my sister out here."

Millie gasped as Mr. Henley belted out a laugh. "You are delusional, Your Grace."

"No. I am merely shrewd. You want the five thousand I have hidden inside Fournier House? You won't ever find it without me. And I won't help you unless you let Millie out. Now."

He was no longer amused. Baring his teeth, he leaned forward. "Maybe I'll just shoot her instead. She is no longer useful, anyhow."

Beside her, Millie squealed softly and recoiled.

"Harm my sister and you will get nothing. Shoot me and you will get nothing. However, let Millie out here and I will not resist. The money is yours."

His eyes sparked and again, he grated out a dog-like howl. Mr. Henley banged a fist on the wall of the coach. "Pull over!" The horses immediately began to slow. "It seems your sister shall take your place, Lady Redding."

Millie grabbed Audrey's hands. "No, I won't let you."

"It will be just fine, Millie, I promise," Audrey said, though she was almost certain that it, too, was a lie.

"I can't have you walking back to Greenbriar just yet, Lady Redding. We need a better head start if we're to make it to Hertfordshire without interference," Mr. Henley said as the coach drew to a stop. "A leg wound should do nicely."

"No!" Audrey and Millie both screamed as he shifted his pistol toward Millie's shins.

"Guv!" the driver called back. "A rider, coming up behind us."

"*Quiet*," Mr. Henley warned them, though Millie continued to cry and shake violently. He couldn't very well shoot now—the approaching rider would surely stop. "Hush, the pair of you—"

An object came sailing through the open carriage window and struck Mr. Henley in the face. He cried out, his whole body jerking back—and his pistol fired. Searing pain lit up Audrey's thigh and she screamed, but the pain wasn't enough to detract her attention from the blood gushing from their captor's nose. Or the fact that he had lost his grip on the pistol as he wailed in agony.

"Millie! Go!" she cried, reaching for the door. The movement bolted hot pain through her, but she ignored it—especially when a second projectile smashed into Mr. Henley's bleeding face. He rocked back with another roar of pain. A horse and rider then galloped past the coach in a blur—and with a stroke of wonder, Audrey recognized them, for there were *two* riders: Carrigan and Sir!

"Jump!" Audrey gave her sister a shove between her shoulder blades, and Millie's arms went up as she fell to the ground, a few feet below. She landed on her side in a lump.

"Stop!" Mr. Henley screamed. The last thing Audrey saw before she jumped out through the open door was the enraged man scrambling to pick up his pistol.

She landed on the road, her ankle rolling and nearly sending her to the ground next to Millie. The excruciating pain in her thigh threatened to turn her legs to rubber. Millie, however, got to her feet and hooked Audrey's arm over her shoulders. "Hurry!" she cried, then screamed again as the driver leaped down from the box in front of them, blocking their path.

"Duck, duchess!" came Sir's screeching order from close

behind them. They crouched, pain ripping through Audrey's leg, and immediately, the driver toppled backward as something struck him just as it had Mr. Henley. A rock dropped to the dirt, and Audrey realized what Sir was wielding: a slingshot.

"Into the woods!" Carrigan shouted to them as Audrey and Millie stood straight again. The driver rolled on the dirt with his hands clamped around his bloodied eye. Mr. Henley lunged from the open coach door and slammed bodily into both Carrigan and Sir. Audrey's heart dropped.

"Sister, hurry!" Millie cried, and then tugged her off the roadside and into the trees.

CHAPTER

EIGHTEEN

A cluster of servants milled around the open front door to Greenbriar when at last, after an hour of hard riding from Pyke-on-Wending, the house came into view. Hugh, covered in dust and drenched in sweat, dismounted before bringing his horse to a full stop. His instincts had proved correct: something untoward had happened here. The whole ride, he'd felt as though he was not moving fast enough. If he could but fly to Greenbriar—to Audrey—he would have.

She had the ring. She'd had it all along. Lady Redding had been traveling to Greenbriar to fetch it because that was where she had hidden it. Not at Greenbriar itself, but within the large nautilus shell Audrey had treasured since her brother had given it to her when she was a young girl. Hugh recalled it; polished to a mother-of-pearl gleam, the shell had intricate woodland etchings. He recalled the reverent way Audrey held it, her fingers tracing her late brother's artistic endeavors. Cartwright had explained Millie's reasoning for choosing the nautilus, and it made sense. Audrey would care for the shell, and in turn, the ring.

Once, Millie had seen Audrey unpacking the shell from a compartment inside her writing box at Haverfield. She'd realized then that her sister did not leave the nautilus in one place but took it with her wherever she stayed. As Audrey had been staying at Greenbriar for most of the summer, Millie knew it would be with her.

And now, Henley had discovered it as well.

"What is amiss, Munson?" Fournier asked as he met his butler.

"Your Grace, it appears the dowager duchess and Mr. Robert Henley have left Greenbriar together."

Hugh's next step faltered even as his mind charged forward.

Fournier swore under his breath. "Do you know where they have gone?"

"Francis was posted at the door when he heard the gentleman mention something about a turn through the gardens, but they cannot be located," Munson explained. "And then, Lord Neatham's young assistant and Her Grace's driver set off on horseback, shouting to Francis to fetch help."

A sliver of hope buoyed Hugh's sinking stomach. Sir and Carrigan had at least gone after them.

Hugh took the footman currently looking like a kicked dog for Francis. "Did the boy say anything else? Fetch help to where?"

"He only said the duchess had been taken, milord, and to send help down the post road toward Hertfordshire."

Hugh returned to his horse and mounted swiftly. "When was this?"

"No more than half an hour since, milord."

Hugh cracked the reins and started away as Fournier barked orders to his butler to send for Sir Ridley immediately. Hugh tore down the lane, and the pounding of hooves behind him indicated Thornton and Cartwright had followed. Soon, the duke galloped up alongside him as well.

"Are they going to Fournier Downs?" he shouted over the thunder of their horses.

"They must be," Hugh replied. And Henley had to have employed a threat against Millie in order to convince Audrey to leave without a fuss.

He'd turned it over in his mind endlessly as they rode from Lord Montague's lodge: What would Henley's move be? Sneaking into the house and searching Audrey's bedchamber would be too risky, especially during the day when servants were coming and going from the guests' rooms. Henley had given his regrets, but what if he simply arrived late, surprising his hostess and those who had looked forward to hearing about their investments? Then, he might corner Audrey...force her into her bedchamber and coerce her to hand over the shell. If she had, and he'd taken Audrey from Greenbriar to dispose of her elsewhere...

Hugh vibrated with fury and fear. He dug in his heels and urged the tired horse onward. There hadn't been time to change out their mounts for fresh ones, but at this pace, if Henley had less than a half hour's head start, they would soon catch up.

Perhaps Audrey had drawn Henley away from Greenbriar purposefully. All her things were still in her room, and in all probability the writing box too, as her journey back to Hertfordshire had been interrupted. She may have lied to him to avoid having to hand the ring over, which would have effectively ended any use she or Millie were to Henley. Thank god Sir had taken Hugh's instruction to heart, as usual. Before leaving for Pyke-on-Wending, he'd pulled the boy aside and told him not to let the dowager duchess out of his sight. At the time, he'd had Westbrook in mind. After the incident in the library alcove, Hugh would not put it past the churlish man to retaliate in some way. Sir must have seen Henley and Audrey leaving, and then fetched Carrigan's help.

Sweat dampened his skin, causing his shirt to stick and his jacket to feel like it was on fire. Need and panic coiled through him as he pulled ahead of the others. For several minutes, he was only aware of the road ahead. They passed a farmer and his cart, who stared in alarm as they charged past, but no one else. When at last he saw a black coach stopped on the side of the road ahead, Hugh finally drew breath. His lungs ached as if it was the first he'd drawn in ages.

"That is Henley's coach," Cartwright said.

Hugh drew his flintlock from its holster only a moment before seeing a strange lump writhing on the ground near the stopped coach. A man.

Their mounts circled the empty coach, its door open. On a bench seat inside, Hugh spied a tangle of rope. The man peeled himself off the ground and staggered toward a loose horse, skittishly prancing near the abandoned coach.

"Hold!" Fournier commanded.

Thornton rode between the man and the horse. "Where is Henley?"

The man turned to run away, but they promptly encircled him. A gash in his forehead bled profusely, and his eye had swollen shut.

"Speak up, man," Fournier said.

"Where are the others?" Hugh demanded. The man only gaped. Hugh dismounted and was about to take him by the lapels when a shout sounded through the thick woods beside the road.

"In there," Hugh said, then for good measure, pummeled the ruffian in the jaw. The man dropped to the road. "Cartwright, tie him up. There's rope in the carriage. Thornton, Fournier, with me."

He signaled for quiet as they darted into the trees. When he'd been younger, he'd tracked deer in the forest around Cranleigh with his father. He'd learned to look for disturbances—broken twigs, impressions in the ground, ripped bark. With no more sounds emanating from the woods, he looked for evidence of where Audrey and Henley had gone. Carrigan and Sir too, as the skittish horse was surely the mount the two had ridden from Greenbriar. With so many feet tramping through the woods here, he found plenty of disturbance, and soon, voices reached him. They were inaudible at first, but Audrey's familiar voice restarted his heart and sharpened his focus.

He raised his hand, then indicated Thornton and Fournier to split apart, as they had at Montague Lodge, to circle around the people ahead. Hugh went forward alone. A few more strides and the voices became clear. Movement rippled between tree trunks.

"There is no money hidden at Fournier Downs, is there? You were lying."

Henley, Hugh presumed, heaving for breath as though he'd just finished sprinting. Careful not to snap a stick underfoot and give away his approach, Hugh inched closer.

A woman sat in a small clearing on the forest floor, pressed against a fallen log and cradling her knee. He recognized Lady Redding from her portrait at Haverfield. Audrey and Carrigan stood in front of her. The way Audrey clung to Carrigan, her driver supporting her around her waist, concerned him. She'd been hurt. Sir fought with Audrey's outstretched arm as she attempted to push him behind them. The boy was attempting to shield her.

Henley's back was to Hugh, but he could still see the pistol he aimed at the foursome. A double barrel flintlock, like Hugh's own. He'd have, at most, two bullets in his weapon. Hugh moved, and Audrey's eyes flared as she spotted him.

"I did lie," she said, her attention snapping back to Henley. "We were steps away from the ring at Greenbriar, and yet your desperation was so extreme, you allowed me to lead you from it."

Her intent was obvious, at least to Hugh. She wanted to inflame Henley, pull his attention from the woods surrounding them as Hugh positioned himself closer. It worked.

"Devious bitch!" he shouted.

Hugh moved out from the trees and pulled the first hammer back on his flintlock. "Drop your weapon."

Henley froze, but he did not lower the pistol.

"He has one shot left," Audrey said, wincing as she shifted her footing. Her black skirt sported a darker patch. Blood. Had the bastard shot her?

"You're finished, Henley," he said. "We've found Cartwright. He's told us everything."

"Has he, now?" Henley grated out a laugh. "This is all his doing."

"*You* were taken in by a swindler, not Cartwright," Hugh said. "You unintentionally defrauded your peers, and this is how you remedy your mistakes? Kidnapping, murder, and theft?"

"If I had been heir, this would have never happened!" Henley's flustered exclamation frightened some birds from the limbs of the trees around them. Just then, Thornton and Fournier emerged on opposite sides of the clearing.

"I had to invest. Grandfather squandered everything, his allowance to me dwindled to a pittance," he spat.

"Heir or not, you'd possess the same spoiled character," Cartwright said, having reached them. Henley, his pistol still aimed at his captives, turned his head just enough to glimpse his cousin.

"He did it all on purpose, you know. He hated you so much that he was prepared to ruin his own legacy so that you would get nothing."

Hugh didn't think this was a lie. The sorry state of Montague's country seat and the rumors of his depleted wealth, not to mention his disappearance from society, supported Henley's claims.

"Then he has labored in vain," Cartwright said. "I never planned to use a farthing of his money to do anything but keep up the estate. I have made my own fortune without handouts from him, and without cheating decent people, as you have." He sighed, resignation and disappointment weighting it. "You are just as cruel and hollow-hearted as he is. You are right, cousin. You truly should have been heir."

Henley sneered and flexed his hand—and Hugh anticipated the man's next move a bare second before Henley spun on his heel.

"Audrey, down!" he shouted, knowing she would be in his own line of fire.

Henley swung his pistol toward Cartwright, intending to use his last shot on the object of his envy. Simultaneously, Audrey threw herself on top of Millie, Carrigan tackled Sir to the ground, and Hugh fired. Henley's pistol discharged, but the shot went into the ground as he staggered forward. He dropped to a knee, then fell sideways into some ferns.

Cartwright stared, wide-eyed at his fallen cousin, belatedly realizing he would have been shot. Hugh surged toward Audrey. She slowly rose from atop her sister, just as Sir shoved Carrigan off with muffled complaints.

Hugh dropped to Audrey's side and cupped her cheeks, barely resisting the urge to kiss her. "You're injured."

"My leg," she confirmed just as her sister cried, "She's been shot!"

Hugh twisted. "Thornton!"

His friend was already there, shoving Hugh out of the way. Tossing modesty to the wind, Thornton raised her skirt's hem, exposing cream silk stockings, garters, and drawers. Hugh's stomach lurched at the crimson soaked into them. As Thornton deftly inspected Audrey's thigh, Cartwright helped Millie to her feet and away.

"He was going to shoot me, but then something came through the window and struck the horrible wretch in the face," Millie gasped as she clung to Cartwright, tears streaming down her cheeks.

"It were a rock," Sir said with a proud nod. He held his slingshot high. "A good sized one too."

Carrigan removed his jacket and ripped the sleeve of his shirt, tearing the threads at the shoulder seam. "Here, use this." He handed the strip of cloth to Thornton, who took it and wrapped it around Audrey's thigh. He tied it off in a knot, and when she answered with a gasp of pain, her cheeks draining of color, Hugh gritted his teeth. "Well? Her leg, Thornton, do you need to remove the bullet?"

"No. It seems to only be a deep graze. Sutures will be necessary, but it can wait until we are back at Greenbriar. You will be just fine, Your Grace."

Hugh closed his eyes with relief, and Audrey leaned against him, her head resting against his chest. As she took deep breaths, he gave up resisting and brushed his lips to her forehead. He didn't care who saw what.

"What about Mr. Faradiddles here?" Sir asked, gesturing toward Henley, who had indeed been brimming over with all his lies. He lay unmoving in the ferns. Fournier crouched and rolled him over. A moment later, he shook his head.

"Dead."

Hugh disregarded the clenching in his chest. In all the years he'd been a Bow Street officer, he'd only shot and killed one man—his own half-brother, Thomas. Now, Henley. He did not regret what had needed to be done. Had Henley lived, he would have only been sent to the noose anyhow.

"Come." Hugh wrapped his arms around Audrey and lifted her to her feet, though she hissed and moaned when she finally stood. "Hold onto my neck," he instructed, and then as gently as possible, hooked her legs, lifted them, and cradled her in his arms.

"I can walk." Her protest was predictable. She hated being vulnerable. Despised admitting she was fragile. But she was. As strong and fierce and courageous as she was, she was far from impervious. His desire to protect her, shield her, had only increased since their night together. And yet, he also knew she would never have permitted such mollycoddling had she not been bleeding from a gunshot wound.

"I know you can," he told her. "You are a marvel. But even marvels need assistance once in a while."

She opened her mouth, to object again, most likely. But Lady Redding cut her off.

"Let the viscount carry you, sister." She glanced over Cartwright's shoulder as he guided her into the woods, toward the road, and smiled warmly at Audrey. "You've been brave enough for one day."

NINETEEN

"Why is this so much worse than when I was shot in the shoulder?"

Audrey's fingers, laced with Hugh's, squeezed as Lord Thornton made a final suture and knotted the thin black floss. While she'd seen the deep, angry path the bullet had made along her outer thigh during Lord Thornton's thorough cleaning of the area, and knew the injury was a mere four-inch graze—an extremely lucky graze that could have been far worse—her whole leg burned and throbbed.

"I suspect it is because you are conscious this time," the physician said, glancing up from his work with a wry arch of his brow.

When she'd been shot in the shoulder at the Thames, the bullet had torn through, front to back before she'd plunged into cold water. She'd been near delirious when Hugh had delivered her to St. James's Square, into the care of his trusted friend.

"I think you must be correct," she said, at least grateful the suturing process was now over.

Nausea had made her dizzy, and she collapsed against Hugh's side, shivering in a cold sweat as Lord Thornton next began wrapping clean cotton linen around her thigh. She and Hugh sat on her bed at Greenbriar, with Lord Thornton perched on the edge as he worked. Hugh had held her the entire time the wound had been cleaned and stitched. Lord Thornton had cleared the room of all but Greer, who had refused to leave and instead, dutifully assisted with bringing hot water, clean cloths, and fetching certain items from Lord Thornton's medical bag.

Audrey's ruined stockings and drawers had been removed for the procedure, and her skirt positioned as modestly as possible, but she was unexpectedly at ease with Lord Thornton's ministrations. If Hugh trusted him explicitly, then so would she.

"There," Lord Thornton said, finishing with the cotton linen. "That will need changing tomorrow morning. I will check on the state of the sutures then. We will also watch for a fever. But I am confident you will heal well, Your Grace."

Audrey reached for his hand as he made to stand. "Please, call me Audrey."

He glanced at Hugh briefly, as if seeking approval, and then nodded. "With pleasure. And I would be honored if you would call me Grant," he said, then cocked a sly grin. "Though generally, I *am* on first name terms with every patient I've treated north of the ankle."

It might have been the pain or the release of tension, but his quip brought out a spate of giddy laughter.

"All right, all right," Hugh said when she failed to smother it. "He isn't that humorous."

A knock landed on the closed door to the bedchamber

and when it opened, Cassie swept inside, concern etched on her stricken face. "It's been ages," she said. "How is she?"

Lord Thornton stood and plunged his hands into the basin of water on the bedside table as Cassie hurried toward the bed.

"There is no need to worry, I promise," Audrey said as she lowered her skirt to cover the wrapped thigh.

"Her Grace was very lucky," Lord Thornton said while drying off his hands.

Audrey knew it was true. Mr. Henley had been about to shoot Millie in the leg when Sir's rock had come sailing through the window and his pistol had discharged without aim. That bullet could have gone into one of their hearts or heads.

Cassie let out a long exhale as the worry that had plainly been torturing her lifted. Perhaps the same sudden and giddy relief that had caused Audrey to laugh at Lord Thornton's teasing comment was to blame for what Cassie did next: She went to the physician and threw her arms around him in an embrace. Lord Thornton stood rigidly, the towel still grasped in his hand and surprise searing his expression.

"Oh, am I so relieved, I—" Cassie cut herself off as she seemed to realize what she was doing. She leaped away from him, a fine blush rising to her cheeks. "Oh. I'm sorry, I…" She cleared her throat. "I'm just pleased a physician was at Greenbriar to help."

Her eyes wide with humiliation, Cassie gave her back to Thornton and came to Audrey. She sat on the side of the bed, her spine rigid. Audrey bit back a chuckle as the open bedchamber door filled again, this time with Michael and Millie. Hugh shifted straighter on the bed at her side.

Michael's keen attention did not overlook the intimate hold of his arm wrapped around Audrey's shoulder, but he didn't address it. Millie observed as well, her lips pressing into a small grin. She wore a new dress, likely taken from her luggage that had been left in her abandoned coach, and her hair had been re-pinned.

"Sir Ridley has arrived," Michael announced. "He would like a word with you, Neatham. And you, Thornton."

Hugh shifted again on the bed, slipping his arm out from behind her.

"I won't be long," he told her. Then, as he'd done in the woods, he kissed her forehead. When he pulled away, his eyes were bright with mischief. He knew exactly how improper it was to show such affection, and yet he did not care.

As he stood and joined Lord Thornton and Michael, who now arched a brow in disapproval, Audrey thought her cheeks must resemble Cassie's pink flush. Although, her sister-in-law seemed to have discarded her own embarrassment in favor of grinning smugly at Audrey.

"I knew it," she whispered as the men left the room. Audrey shook her head.

"We must change your dress, Your Grace," Greer said, smoothing over the awkward moment.

The black frock was ruined, having snagged on thorn bushes on top of being shredded by a bullet and stained with blood.

"I wonder if I might first have a moment with my sister," Millie said, her hands clasped before her. "It won't take but a few minutes."

Audrey nodded to Greer, who bobbed a curtsey and left the room. Cassie also stood. "I will let Genie know how you're feeling. She's been occupied with trying to calm Lady Kettleridge. The woman nearly fainted when she heard Mr. Henley shot you."

"Lord Kettleridge will no doubt be just as faint when he learns he's been fleeced," Audrey said. She did feel sorry for him and Mr. Filmore for their lost investments. She supposed she should also feel sorry for Lord Westbrook, but the man was so disagreeable, it was difficult to feel pity.

"At any rate, I fear the house party has come to an early end," Cassie said as she moved toward the door. "Lady Veronica has already directed her maid to begin packing her things."

"Such a shame," Audrey replied. They shared a grin before Cassie saw herself out.

The bedchamber grew suddenly empty and quiet. At the same time, the remaining person filled the room considerably.

"The viscount is in love with you," Millie said.

Audrey inhaled and held her breath, waiting for her sister to say more. Express disapproval and reproach. But she didn't. She only waited for Audrey's response.

"Yes," she replied. "He is."

Kissing her forehead like that in front of everyone had all but announced that after her mourning period had ended, a happy announcement could be expected.

Her sister's expression remained open and friendly. Something Audrey was not in the least accustomed to.

She braced for pain as she shifted her legs off the edge of the bed. Her feet touched the floor, and Millie rushed to her side.

"What are you doing? You should stay in bed and rest."

"This will only take a moment," Audrey said, extending her arm. Millie took it. "Help me to the desk?"

She looped Audrey's arm over her shoulders and held her by the waist as she stood, putting most of her weight on her good leg. It still ached and burned like fire, but she was too eager to reach her writing box and ignored the pain as she and Millie shuffled across the room. The box, crafted of polished cherry wood, brass fittings, and a brass plate engraved with her initials, had been a gift from Audrey's late grandmother. She'd asked Greer to unpack it from her trunk when her stay at Greenbriar had been extended.

Audrey released herself from Millie's helpful hold, lowered herself into the desk's chair, and reached for the clasp. Springing the lid, she saw the flat shelf inside, which held a stack of writing papers of different sizes. She lifted the shelf to access the bottom of the box, where smaller compartments held an ink bottle, pens and nibs, blotting papers— and the object of Mr. Henley's greedy desire.

She scooped up the nautilus shell, its shape and weight familiar in the palm of her hand. She'd memorized the etchings James had worked into the polished exterior long ago and had thought she knew everything there was to know about the shell. She would often peer up into the main chamber, but nothing had ever caught her eye inside.

Audrey held it out to Millie, who took the shell carefully, as if touching something fragile. She turned it over and with a trembling hand, reached her thumb and forefinger high into the opening. After a moment, she let out a little gasp, and then withdrew a balled-up scrap of blue chamois. She set the shell back into Audrey's palms, and then unwrapped the soft fabric, revealing one of the loveliest gemstones Audrey had ever seen.

The large, square cut diamond was a vivid lilac purple, the brilliant shimmer of its facets mesmerizing in the sunset light that was now slanting through the window. The gold setting and band had tarnished during the years the ring had been hidden inside the shell, but the stone was flawless.

"Oh my," she said, gazing at the diamond. "I think I underestimated its worth. It would surely fetch more than the five thousand I told Mr. Henley."

Millie rubbed the soft chamois along the tarnished band. "You were remarkable. I never would have thought to trick him in such a way. I was far too terrified."

"I was scared, too," Audrey admitted. "I only wanted to give us some time."

Millie, still focused on her task of polishing the band, sniffled. Her voice caught. "You were trying to save me."

She sounded stunned that Audrey would have done so.

"We are sisters, are we not?"

"I haven't been a good one to you."

"Millie—"

"No, please. Let me speak." She set the ring onto the desk and paced a few steps away. "When our mother and uncle rejected Reggie's proposal, I didn't fight. I didn't do anything except bend to their will, to what would make other people more comfortable. I knew the only reason they objected was because of his brown skin. He was the heir to an marquessate, for heaven's sake, and yet they vastly preferred Lord Redding, an old, white viscount." She balled her hands into fists. "I was so engrossed in my own life and my own bitterness that I...I looked the other way when I learned you had been sent to that horrible place. I told myself I had my own worries."

By that time, Millie had been married and a mother. She *had* had her own worries. Audrey said as much, but Millie shook her head tightly.

"I was a coward," she blurted out. "A bitter coward, afraid to stand up to our bully of a mother and our equally horrible uncle. I only cared about pleasing her, even if deep down I knew no one, least of all me, would ever be able to accomplish such a feat."

Audrey listened, fascinated. She had never so much as questioned if her sister felt this way toward their mother and uncle.

"I always thought you were like her," Audrey said, and at Millie's pained flinch, added, "But you're not. I see that now. I'm sorry I was blind."

Millie shook her head and laughed, though the sound was stunted by the oncoming of tears. "Oh, no. You weren't blind. I made certain to push you away."

"But why?"

Millie let her fingers drift toward the ring, but she didn't touch it. "I remember well when you broke your betrothal to Lord Bainbury. It caused such an uproar, and yet you didn't let it stop you. You followed your heart. I was envious." She shrugged. "But I was envious of you long before that. James, he was so smitten with you. So was Papa. You dominated all their attention."

Audrey reached for her sister's hand. She held it without saying anything.

"I felt so small and petty today when you threw yourself in front me and tried to protect me. When I heard how much you'd done to try to find me." Millie's tears spilled over. "I want to make it up to you, but I don't know how."

Audrey winced as she stood, bracing herself against the desk and taking her weight off her injured leg.

"You can start by marrying the man you love." She squeezed her sister's hand. "That is still Lord Cartwright, if I'm not mistaken?"

Millie wiped her tears, her smile glittering despite her wet cheeks and stuffy nose from crying. "Oh, yes. It is. I've only ever loved Reggie."

"Then start anew with him. It isn't too late."

"Mother and uncle will be furious." She hitched her chin. "But I don't care anymore."

Audrey felt the sting of tears coming on too. It was all too much. Her sister, always so staid and proper and disparaging...had seemed to transform right before Audrey's eyes. She tried to divert the emotion by picking up the diamond ring and handing it to Millie.

"You'll need this then."

Millie turned it over in her palm. "My, but it is ostentatious, isn't it? I'm not sure I can wear it, knowing that my maid was killed because of it."

"The ring isn't at fault. Your maid was killed by Mr. Henley in an act of immoral desperation. She was tricked. I'm sure she regretted it dearly before...before she died."

And Samuel, the valet, too. He must have informed Mr. Henley of the ring when it became apparent that he'd been swindled by this silver mine con-artist. If he had not breathed a word about it for fifteen years, something serious had to have driven him to do so. But he had misjudged his employer and had likely dug himself a hole he could not rise out of.

The other few brutish accomplices had merely been hired ruffians, according to the driver Lord Cartwright had tied up.

Audrey closed Millie's fingers around the ring. "Even if you don't wear the ring, it is a symbol. Lord Cartwright never stopped loving you. He knew that one day you'd be together."

Millie swiped at her eyes again to clear the ceaseless tears. "I don't deserve your kindness, Audrey."

"Nonsense. You're starting anew with *Reggie*," she said, playfully attempting to tease her sister. But then grew more serious. "I don't see why we can't as well?"

Millie took a shaky breath. She squeezed Audrey's hand, still clasped in her own, once more, and then released it to smooth the front of her skirt.

"When Reggie and I return from our wedding trip, I insist you come stay with us. I would like you to get to know your nieces and nephews."

Audrey blinked back tears, but not so successfully this time. "I would like nothing more."

TWENTY

The promise of autumn had been on the air the last few mornings as Audrey prepared to leave Greenbriar. A fortnight had passed since the dramatic events that saw Millie and Lord Cartwright rescued, Mr. Henley killed, and Audrey wounded by a bullet—once again. Genie and Cassie had not been the only ones to insist she stay on in Kent while her leg wound healed; Michael had all but demanded it. He pretended not to have been affected by the violent encounter with Mr. Henley, citing numerous battles on the Continent against the French, but Audrey knew her brother-in-law well, and he couldn't completely hide that it had shaken him.

"You will stay here, under my roof, until all danger has passed," he had commanded, the last few words squeezed by emotion tightening his throat. She'd been touched by his concern, even if Lord Thornton—or Grant, as he'd invited her to call him—had deemed her to be healing well and in no danger of complications from the wound. She would survive, he said with a wink the following morning.

The house party, however, had not.

Genie's guests started leaving in a flurry after breakfast the next day, which Audrey had insisted on attending, even though her leg pained her. Lady Kettleridge had peppered her with inquiries about Mr. Henley's duplicity, being abducted from Greenbriar and shot, and "all this business having to do with a diamond ring" until her husband had erupted from his silence to tell her to hush. He and Lord Westbrook appeared ragged at the breakfast table, as if they'd had too little sleep and far too much whisky the night before while Hugh and Michael had been informing them of their losses in the non-existent silver mine. Mr. Filmore, however, had tapped the crown of his soft-boiled egg at breakfast and tucked into his honey cake and tea with only a fraction of his companions' disappointment.

"The nature of speculation, I'm afraid," he'd said with a sad shake of his head. "Henley made a grave mistake throwing everything he had into a mine he had not seen for himself and with a man he had just met. No, no, you only risk what you can afford to lose. That is what I always advise."

Lords Kettleridge and Westbrook had glared at Mr. Filmore from their seats, their breakfast plates untouched. Audrey suspected the two lords had not followed Mr. Filmore's rule of thumb and had lost significantly.

Lady Veronica had not been at breakfast, and Audrey had not seen her before she and her mother hastened to their carriage and left Greenbriar before the noon hour. Later, Cassie had enthusiastically informed her that Veronica had all but snubbed Hugh when taking her leave.

"It appears she has been made to understand that Lord

Neatham will not be making her an offer," Cassie had said with an impish smirk.

Audrey found it difficult to feel sorry for the debutante. She'd been so unpleasant and competitive, when all along, she'd had no chance of winning Hugh's affections. Audrey let go of her irritation with Lady Veronica, and instead felt silly for being envious of her in the first place.

Mrs. Stewart and her daughter had been less inquisitive of the drama and dealings with Mr. Henley and more concerned with Audrey's and Millie's welfare, which Audrey had appreciated. Though Cassie was still prickly around Cynthia, Audrey didn't believe she wholly disliked the young woman. It was more likely that Cassie was attempting to stem the comparisons she was making in her own mind between herself and the woman whom William had turned to. However, after her awkward embrace with Grant Thornton, Cassie had seemed less concerned with Cynthia and more concerned with avoiding the physician.

Though Grant had stayed on another week, to remove the stitches from her thigh, Hugh had come and gone during that time. He'd been helping Sir Ridley with the inquest into Mr. Henley's crimes and death and explaining the details of the events to an emergency convening of the House of Lords in London. He'd also spent a few days attempting to track down Mr. Teague. The account at the London bank where Mr. Henley deposited the invested funds had been cleared out, and the luxurious rooms Mr. Teague had been leasing had been abandoned. It was unlikely he was still in the country, Hugh had informed her when he'd returned to Greenbriar. Or that his name was even Teague.

Though Hugh had sat slumped and exhausted in her

bedchamber chair, covered in road dust and sweat as he described his lack of findings in London, there had been no denying the glimmer of exhilaration too. He'd enjoyed stepping back into his role as an investigator, even if it had not been in an official capacity.

"You miss it," she'd said, propped as she was in her bed, her leg on a pillow. He'd looked delectably roguish in that chair, his eyes lingering on her for a few prolonged moments. It brought a heated blush to her cheeks.

"I've asked Sir Gabriel to think of me when he's confronted with cases that could be a challenge for his officers," he'd replied. "I hope you aren't opposed to that."

"Why should I be?"

"Because what you think, and what you want, matters to me."

The confession rendered her speechless. When he'd come to perch on the edge of her bed and taken her hand in his, she'd known a happiness so overwhelming it nearly frightened her. Was this what love was? A passion so fierce that it could quickly become her only source of oxygen? In the days Hugh had been gone, he had been on her mind constantly. She'd missed him with a new intensity, too. But she knew she could not lose herself to these powerful feelings.

"I hope you aren't opposed to asking for my assistance," she said. "I want to be your partner, Hugh. In everything."

He'd lifted her hand to his lips, his rich brown eyes penetrating. "You already are. And you always will be."

They'd been interrupted then as Greer had entered the room to draw Audrey a bath. Hugh had stood up, joking that he required one himself. With a flutter of anticipation and wonder, Audrey pictured a not-too-distant future where such an undertaking could be done together, rather than apart.

Now, after a few quiet days at Greenbriar while Audrey continued to strengthen her leg and heal, she and Genie were once again arm-in-arm as they approached the courtyard and a trio of waiting carriages. It was time to depart Kent, and Audrey could only hope they were not waylaid by anything untoward this time.

"Are you sure about this?" Genie asked. "What if your leg bothers you when you're abroad?"

Audrey patted her hand. She was a true mother hen, and it suited her well. Especially now that she had quietly announced to her and Cassie a few days ago at tea that come winter, George was to expect a sibling. Audrey was thrilled at the announcement, and Cassie had been as well. Though, when Genie had turned to ask the maid to bring cakes and lemonade for celebration, Audrey had caught a wistful twinge at the corner of Cassie's smile. Not that she would have ever let Genie see it.

"Cassie, Carrigan, and Greer will take good care of me."

Audrey had put forward the idea to Cassie the week before that they should take the next few months to travel the Continent, and as expected, her sister-in-law leaped at the invitation. The trip wasn't entirely to avoid London society, though it did play a large role. She simply couldn't fathom staying at Violet House the next nine months while she waited out the rest of her mourning period. The solitude and boredom would drive her to the brink of madness. And Cassie, with no desire at all to attend any social events or find a husband during the upcoming Little Season, saw it as the perfect excuse to escape.

"You must write often," Genie said, and then softer, "and keep an eye on her. I think she is very unhappy, though she tries to conceal it."

Next to her own waiting carriage, Cassie stood patiently listening to Michael as he no doubt tried to talk her out of leaving for the Continent and instead staying to find a husband. Behind him, out of his view, Tobias rolled his eyes, at which Cassie's lips thinned in an attempt not to laugh.

"I agree," Audrey said. "I think traveling will occupy her thoughts. Perhaps it will even inspire a change of heart."

It would also take her far from London and the very handsome and intriguing Lord Thornton. During the week he remained at Greenbriar, Audrey had caught Grant's attention drifting toward Cassie when he thought no one was looking. Cassie, however, avoided even acknowledging that he was in the room, her embarrassment was still so high. While Audrey liked Grant very much, and he was Hugh's closest friend, he was far too old for Cassie. He had to be in his early thirties and his reputation for being a rake and mixing with the demimonde was well known.

"I should go rescue her from my tyrant of a husband," Genie said, then kissed Audrey's cheeks and gave her a quick embrace. "Besides, I think someone is looking for your undivided attention."

Following her coy glimpse, Audrey saw Hugh waiting next to her carriage. His own was the third in courtyard, laden with luggage and already filled with his young assistant and valet. They were on their way to Surrey for the remainder of September before they would return to London.

Hugh wore sable buckskins and black hessians, and a

green swallow-tailed coat over a deep green embroidered waistcoat that seemed to be a favorite of his. Either that, or it was a favorite of Basil's and Hugh merely relented to his valet's imperious will.

As she approached him, Audrey prepared herself. She hadn't been looking forward to this moment, and by the cheerless set of his mouth, Hugh felt much the same.

"I don't like the idea of you traveling alone," he said as she joined him.

"I won't be alone."

"Yes, I know, you'll have Carrigan." He said it as if by rote memorization. She supposed he'd heard it enough times. It never placated him, though, even if her driver had proved to be stalwart in his protection.

Right then, Carrigan and Greer were locked in a conversation near the horses, and her maid's lips were curiously drawn into a grin. The expression was so foreign to Audrey that she had to look twice to believe it.

"I will also have Cassie," she reminded Hugh. Then, thinking of her earlier suspicions, she decided to ask him point-blank, "Do you think Grant has developed an interest in her?"

Surprise transformed his gloomy face, and he all but laughed at the suggestion. "Thornton? I would not give Lady Cassandra any hope there."

"Hope? I'm of the opinion it's a bad idea."

Now Hugh's scowl returned. "I thought you liked him. Well enough to call him *Grant*."

She secretly enjoyed the minor show of jealousy. He had commented more than once on the two of them now being on first name terms, and before leaving Greenbriar, Grant had playfully fanned the flames of Hugh's irritation any chance he got. Audrey had not taken his flirtations to heart, though she feared Cassie might, if the physician's ever turned his charm toward her.

"I do like him, but he is...well, on top of being much older, I fear he is..."

"A scoundrel?" Hugh provided.

Hearing him say it made her feel slightly guilty. "Not entirely that, but he does have a mildly libertine reputation."

Hugh shook his head. "Thornton knows better than to dally with Lady Cassandra, and I'm afraid that's all he is good for. His love for his late wife continues to have a hold on him."

"Oh." Her sympathy for the physician rushed forward. Now she felt even more shamefaced. "I didn't know."

"He loved Sarah fiercely." Hugh held her stare, his eyes turning dusky. The intensity of his gaze changed. Though he stood an arm's length away, and he didn't reach for her, she could sense his urge to touch her. To hold her and kiss her. And more.

He lowered his voice. "I didn't understand what he felt, not truly. I do now."

Audrey longed for a moment alone with him. They'd had so few since his return from Town. A few stolen kisses—one in the glasshouse, while they waited out a rain shower, had made her legs turn to putty and her good sense fizzle.

If they had been alone now, she would have taken his hand and assured him that she would be safe on her trip to the Continent. It was worrying him; she could see it as he thought of Grant and the loss he'd suffered.

"Will you see him?" Hugh asked. The question confused

her. She frowned, not understanding until he added, "On your travels."

Philip. He meant *Philip*. Her lungs emptied and disappointment flooded her. "Is that what you think I'm doing? Going to the Continent to see him?"

She leaned backward in dismay. He chased her with a step forward despite their present company, occupied though they were in conversation.

"No." But then he sighed and admitted, "I wondered if it had crossed your mind."

"I was honest with you earlier. I have no idea," she curtailed her voice, "where he is. America for all I know."

Contrition crossed his face and Hugh nodded. "I'm sorry. I know you were being honest. I suppose I just don't like that you'll be so far away."

"We've been apart before," she reminded him, releasing her disappointment. "For months at a time, if memory serves."

"I'm ready for that pattern to end," he grumbled.

She bit her lip and grinned. "As am I."

He squared his shoulders, which had started to slump in a boyish pout. Now, however, he appeared his usual, unassailable self. "How will I find you?"

"I will write and keep you updated on where I am," she promised.

"Good. And take care—you have a tendency to find trouble."

She gaped at him in an imitation of shock. "On the contrary, Lord Neatham, I think it is trouble that tends to find me."

"I'm not convinced that is any better."

Just then, Carrigan and Greer parted ways and her driver stepped forward. "Are you ready to depart, Your Grace? We should leave soon if we're to make it to Town before nightfall."

"Just a moment," she replied.

Cassie, too, was giving her goodbyes to her brothers and Genie. She and her maid would be going to Grosvenor Square to pack her things for their trip. Audrey would send notice to the hotel in Paris where she and Philip stayed on their wedding trip, to reserve accommodations. And then, they would all set out for Dover the following week before crossing the Channel to Calais.

It would be months before Audrey set eyes on Hugh again. Though she knew this trip was warranted and would make the next months pass by much more swiftly, she hesitated.

"I would kiss you if it weren't for all the eyes on us," she whispered.

Hugh arched a brow and took her gloved hand in his. Ignoring the others, he pressed a kiss to her knuckles, encased in black silk, and kept his eyes hinged on hers. "Soon that won't matter. And I warn you—it will be a very long time before I can keep my mouth off yours, whether people are looking or not."

Audrey felt as if she might incinerate on the spot. Nearby, Michael cleared his throat, and when Hugh handed Audrey up into her carriage, even Carrigan was smothering a grin.

"Dead bodies," Hugh said. "Steer clear of them, will you?"

"I shall certainly try."

238 • CARA DEVLIN

Hugh shut the door and mouthed *"I love you"* before stepping back to join the others.

Audrey kept her tears at bay as Carrigan got into the driver's box, and as she waved to Genie, Michael, Tobias, and their staff that had come out to see them off. As the carriage pulled away, and when she could no longer see Hugh, she sat back and closed her eyes, finally allowing them to slip down her hot cheeks.

"Nothing will change while we are gone, Your Grace," Greer said after a few moments of quiet. Audrey peered at her maid, who wore a knowing look. It wasn't quite a smile, as she had given Carrigan, but close. "We will be back in England before you know it."

"Yes, Greer, you are right," she said, wiping her cheeks.

Hugh would be there when she returned. She would be in half-mourning then, and able to be a bit more social. If Sir Gabriel were to give him a case, she would not have to bow out and sit at home twiddling her thumbs. She was eager for it.

But until then, she would enjoy her trip with Cassie. And with any hope, the trouble Hugh teased her about would stay far, far away.

Thank you for reading Fatal by Design and for continuing the Bow Street Duchess Mystery series! Please consider leaving a rating and review on Amazon to help other readers discover the series. The sixth book in the series, Nature of the Crime, is scheduled to release January 20, 2024, and is available for pre-order now!

NATURE OF THE CRIME

BOOK #6

The next Bow Street Duchess Mystery is releasing Jan. 20, 2024, and is available for pre-order now!

ABOUT THE AUTHOR

Cara is an author, history lover, and Netflix junkie. She loves to read and write across genres, but her heart is reserved for romantic historical fiction and mystery. When she's not writing, she's driving her kids everywhere, burning at least one side of a grilled cheese, or avoiding doing laundry.

Printed in Great Britain
by Amazon